REAL

BETH YARNALL

REAL

ebook ISBN: 9781940811901

print ISBN: 9781940811598

1
———

*O*ption thirty.

Cal had asked her which options were her favorite on their wedding day, and Lucy had listed option thirty last even though it was the one she most wanted to try. After what she'd been forced to tell him, he'd chosen her favorite option instead of one of his own.

She lay on the bed naked, her legs wide for him. He'd placed a chair at the end of the bed, which added an extra dimension she hadn't anticipated.

"Do you trust me, darlin'?"

She nodded, her eyes wider than they'd been before.

"I'm going to sit here. I'm not allowed to move or touch you. I can't touch myself. And you're going to do everything I tell you to do, got that?"

"Yes."

"Good girl. Now we're going to start with you licking your fingers. Rub them over your nipples in small circles.
"

She did as he asked, her nipples pebbling.

"Pinch them."

She took her nipples between her fingers as he'd commanded, feeling the pull deep inside. Arching her back, she pinched harder, letting out a moan.

"I love it when your cheeks flush like that. Do you like it? Do you like touching yourself?"

"Yes," she panted.

"I can tell. Are you pretending it's me, or is it just you?"

"It's me."

"You're so damn sexy, darlin'. You're making me so hard. Feel your body, how soft and voluptuous you are. Your body drives me insane. Are you wet?"

"Yes."

"How wet?"

"Not enough."

"Stroke yourself. Slide your fingers up then down. That's it."

Her breathing grew more rapid. She could see he was enjoying this, the watching. She dipped her fingers down and up, slipping into her slickness, teasing herself. Fully flush with arousal now, all she wanted to do was come.

"Arch your back a little more so the weights pull," he ordered.

She did as he asked, lifting her torso so that the weights tugged her nipples, and it was so close to how it felt when he had his hands on her that she groaned, moving her fingers faster.

"Now pick up the vibrator and switch it on."

The phallus was larger than she would've chosen for herself and had a rabbit-shaped thing at the base. She switched it on, and the ears vibrated.

"The other switch. Turn that on too."

She did, and the beads in the shaft spun while the shaft itself thrust up and down. She gasped in anticipation.

"Slide it inside you. Slowly."

She used the fingers of one hand to widen herself and inserted the vibrator as deep as it would go. She was overwhelmed with sensation. The thrusting action stroked her while the vibrating ears hit just the right spot.

"Look at me, darlin'." He was fully hard, sitting at the edge of the chair, watching her. "Do you know what I see when I look at you?" She shook her head. "I see a woman so unbelievably beautiful and sexual I want to bury myself deep inside you and pound into you until you scream my name. Do it. Move it inside you as I'd move."

She did as she was told, finding a rhythm that rocketed her toward orgasm. Opening her legs wider as the sensations built, she put her other arm above her head, pushing her breasts higher. The clamps bit down, plunging her closer to the edge.

"Faster. Harder. That's it. Fuck yourself. Come for me, darlin'. Come."

The vibration slammed into her from the front as the thrusting head hit her deep, and she went off, throwing her head back and coming so hard she cried out. Never had she felt anything so intense in her life. The orgasm rolled through her, wave after wave of ecstasy. Nothing existed outside of her and the pulsing between her legs. She switched off the vibrator and threw it on the bed. Chest heaving and limbs tingling, she went completely limp.

"Goddammit if that wasn't the hottest thing I've ever seen."

She'd forgotten he was there. She turned her head to

the side so she could look at him. "Thirty is *the best* number."

"I'm going to have it tattooed on my ass."

She laughed. "Oh, man. I needed that."

He got up from the chair, his penis hard and jutting, and lay on his stomach next to her on the bed. He kissed her shoulder right next to her scar. "You're so damn beautiful, darlin', that sometimes I can hardly breathe when I'm with you. Like right now. Your cheeks are pink and you look happy. Are you happy?"

"I think so. If happy is a loose-limbed kind of numb feeling in my arms and legs."

"That's orgasmic happiness."

She looked into his blue eyes and smiled. "Yeah. I think I am happy. More now than I used to be."

"I still have four more options, you know."

"Four." Laughing, she rolled toward him, the nipple clamps making a tinkling sound as she moved. "Are you planning on using them all tonight?"

"No. Just one more."

"Which is that?"

"This is one that I put on the list, but if you're not comfortable with it, then I'll choose another one."

"It's not one where I have to bend ways that normal people don't bend, is it?"

"Nope. It's one we've done before, so I know you can do it."

She thought of all the ways they'd had sex in the past. There were a couple she wasn't so sure if she could revisit.

"What is it?"

"Thirty-three."

"Which is that?"

"It's a really good one. In fact you can leave these on." He lifted the chain of one of the nipple clamps. "I know how much you enjoyed them."

"How does it work?"

"I lay on my back and you straddle me...backward."

The reverse cowgirl. She wasn't sure how she felt about it.

"Or you can face forward if you'd rather," he offered.

He'd chosen number thirty as the first option he'd won. He'd done it for her. The least she could do was try number thirty-three. It would give her that deep penetration she liked without having him directly behind and on top of her. She could set the pace.

"Okay," she said. "I'll try it."

Cal leaned over and kissed her. It took everything he had not to pounce on her and drive into her without any finesse whatsoever. The way she'd come completely unwound, her legs spread, head back, crying out, he'd had to squeeze his dick to keep from coming right then and there. He'd chosen number thirty-three, hoping she could get off the way he knew she liked it best and yet put her in control. His motives weren't entirely altruistic. He'd have a fine view of her ass as she bounced up and down on top of him.

He wound the chain of one of the clamps around his finger, tugging on her nipple, and then sucked on it. She arched back, leaning into him. He ran his hand over her hip and then between her legs. She was still so wet from pleasuring herself that his fingers slipped easily into her. Widening her legs for him, she tilted her pelvis, giving him deeper access. He knew she was getting close to coming again, and damn it, so was he. He'd been on the verge since he'd told her to spread her legs and touch herself.

Fumbling on the nightstand, he located the condom and rolled it on. With no finesse at all, he shifted so that he was between her thighs. He broke off the kiss and looked down at her.

"I don't care what number this is. I want to see your face." He eased himself into her little by little, watching her the whole time, until he was fully seated. "Oh, God. I can't..."

He began to move within her, thrusting without any skill. It had been *so long* since he'd been inside her. She wrapped around him, hugging him to her. He lost track of everything except the feel of her and his impending orgasm. He chased it, driving hard into her until it hit. He threw his head back and grunted, then collapsed in an unceremonious heap on top of her.

As his heart rate slowed and his brain re-fired its engines, he realized she was crying. He pushed himself up and looked down at her. She was smiling, but tears leaked out of her eyes and into her hair.

"Darlin', what's wrong?"

"Nothing's wrong." She sniffed.

"Then why the tears?"

"Because it's been so long since I came during sex. I missed it."

He put his forehead to hers. "Jesus, darlin', don't say things like that."

"It's true. God, Cal. That was so good. I don't care if it was in the option agreement or not. Plain old vanilla missionary sex works just fine for me."

He gave her a gentle kiss. "Me too, darlin'. Me too. Any way I can be inside you works for me."

"I missed you."

"I missed you too."

"I'm counting this as one of your five even though it's probably not in the option agreement."

"Oh, are you?" He rolled them over so she was on top. One of the nipple clamps had fallen off. He released the other one and threw it on the floor, then he bent his head and kissed each of her breasts. God he loved her breasts.

"Yeah."

"So you're making the rules around here now?"

She leaned forward, brushing her nipples across his chest. "Got a problem with that?"

"No, darlin'. When you do that, I don't have any problems at all with that or anything else in the world."

"Could I ask you a favor?"

"You could ask for anything from me right now and I'd likely give it to you."

Her lips curved into the kind of smile she used to give him. Even if she weren't naked and lying on top of him, that smile would get her whatever she wanted. It had been too damn long since he'd seen it.

He cupped her face. "What can I do for you?"

"Can we keep things the way they are?"

"What do you mean?"

"You haven't exactly been subtle about wanting me to share your bed every night. I'm just not sure I'm ready to move across the hall."

"We can keep them any way you want. I kind of like having to walk across the hall and ask permission to come into my wife's bedroom. Keeps me honest."

"Are you sure?"

"There's only one thing I'm completely sure of, darlin'. And that's if nothing at all changed between us and we stayed exactly the way we are right now, I wouldn't have a thing to complain about."

"You're only saying that because I'm naked and laying on top of you."

"Like I said. Keeps me honest."

2

It was the night of the dinner party when Lucy would really earn her stripes as Cal Seller's wife. She'd chosen what she thought was the perfect dress and had her hair and makeup professionally done. The house was spotless, the decorations flawless. The food was more than delicious—it was exquisite. Even Poppy had a new outfit for the occasion, a cute little red, black, and white dress with white tights and shiny new black Mary Jane shoes.

Lucy stood in the entry hall, ready to greet her husband as he came home from work. She hoped with everything in her that he approved of what she'd done. This dinner was important not only to Cal but to Lucy as well. He'd offered her marriage as a way out of her situation based on her ability to pull off the kind of corporate affairs wives of her caliber were expected to perform. Only she'd never hosted a dinner party, and she'd certainly never choreographed a six-course dinner for four.

Twisting her hands together, she checked the time

again. Twenty minutes. Twenty minutes until their guests arrived, and their host had yet to make an appearance. What would she do if he didn't come home before their guests got here? How would she entertain them?

The front door opened, and Cal appeared. "I'm late. I'll be right down." He barely gave her a glance before he ran past her up the stairs, briefcase in hand.

Halfway up the stairs, he turned. "Damn it." He made his way back down and gave her a brief kiss, then headed upstairs. "I'll be five minutes, no more."

She stared at her husband's retreating form, wishing he was standing next to her so she would at least know what to expect before their guests arrived. She made her way into the kitchen to check yet again on the preparations. All seemed to be in order as the caterer shooed her away. She found herself back in the entryway, alone, waiting for people she'd never met yet had to impress.

She checked her reflection for the third time in the past few minutes. The hairstylist and makeup artist had made her look like someone she hardly recognized, a better, prettier, more presentable version of herself that perfectly matched the expensive dress she wore. She was a long way from the trailer parks and apartment complexes she was used to. Washed, waxed, made up and done up, she felt the part. She knew how to charm people. She knew how to present herself in the best possible light, and she certainly knew which fork to use and when.

She could do this.

Straightening her spine and lifting her chin, she imagined herself greeting the President of the United States and the First Lady. If she was worthy of them, she was certainly worthy of a good old boy from Tennessee and his wife. Even if they were billionaires and were often photographed doing ordinary things like wrangling steer and organic gardening.

Oh, my God.

She was so out of her depth. She didn't know the difference between millionaires and billionaires. To her they were 'aires miles out of her reach. What had Cal been thinking, putting her in charge of a dinner party where she was expected to not only entertain but to charm them over to her side...to Cal's side, where he could convince them he was the one to buy their company and grow their business? She knew *nothing* of these people.

As far as she was concerned they may as well live on opposite sides of the galaxy, let alone the state. She checked her reflection in the hallway mirror for the fourth time. Too much blush! She looked like a harlot. This would never do. She'd embarrass Cal, and the deal would be dead before discussions even began.

She rushed toward the bathroom as Cal thundered down the stairs. He caught up to her halfway there.

"Where are you going?" he asked. "They'll be here any minute."

"I need to fix—" Oh, damn. The doorbell. "I'm wearing too much blush. Stall them." She started for the bathroom again, but he gripped her elbow.

"No, you don't. You look perfect. In fact... Come here."

"There's no time!"

"Darlin', if you don't come here, I'm not going to answer the door.

"*What?*"

"Thought that'd get your attention. Come here." He hooked her hand into the crook of his arm. "You're perfect. Let's greet our guests."

She stared at him like he'd lost his mind because clearly he had, and then the doorbell rang again and she realized it was she who had taken a turn for the worse. She had guests to greet. *Oh, Lord, help me please*, she prayed. There was no way she could get through this night successfully without some kind of divine guidance.

Cal opened the door to a rather ordinary-looking couple about twenty years older than they were. For some reason that made Lucy feel better. The wife's dress was of a similar color as her own, and the man appeared to be more interested in their house than he was either her or Cal.

"Hello, Joel," Cal said smoothly. "This must be your lovely wife, Anne. Please come in."

He held the door open for them. The wife's attention was focused more on Cal than on either her husband or the home they'd been invited into. She spent way too long greeting Cal and hardly gave Lucy a glance as she was introduced. Lucy had her number. Anne Gleason was a woman who had married young for money, produced the proper heirs, and was now free to pursue her options. Lucy was going to make sure that Mrs. Gleason knew that Cal wasn't anyone's option but hers.

"A pleasure to meet you." Lucy held out her hand to Mr. Gleason only to be crushed into a hug so fierce it left her breathless.

"Mrs. Sellers. Lucy," Mr. Gleason said, holding her away from him with both hands on her arms. "I've heard so much about you." His gaze raked her from head to toe, and by the time he was done, Lucy was desperate for a shower.

So this was the man they had to charm into agreeing

to sell his company to Cal's. Cal hadn't mentioned anything to her about him being a letch.

Cal dropped an arm across Lucy's shoulders, drawing her in close. "My wife and I are pleased to welcome you as our first guests as husband and wife. Isn't that right, darlin'?"

Lucy picked up where her husband left off. "It's such a pleasure to have you in our home. Please, won't you come in?" She guided them to the living room where a tray of hors d'oeuvres had already been set up. "May I offer you a drink?"

Mrs. Gleason lowered her shawl, revealing an unexpected plunging neckline. "What do you have?" She settled herself into the sofa, arms draped across the back.

Lucy suddenly realized that Anne's entire outfit was nearly see-through, with little peek-a-boo cutouts that barely covered her areolas. But Mr. Gleason didn't seem to notice his wife's outfit. His eyes were glued to the front of Lucy's dress, which was much more modest in comparison to Mrs. Gleason's.

Lucy sat next to Anne on the couch and crossed her legs.

Instead of sitting in the chair opposite the couch, Mr. Gleason squeezed in next to Lucy, making her scoot over to avoid being sat on.

Cal came forward, reaching a possessive hand out to Lucy. "Darlin', why don't you go and check on dinner while I see to our guests?"

She took his offered hand, leaving Mr. and Mrs. Gleason alone on the couch. "Please, help yourself to an appetizer. I'll be a minute," she told her guests.

Cal followed her partway to the kitchen and leaned

down close to her ear. "You stay next to me and we'll be just fine."

Lucy wasn't so sure. The Gleasons seemed to have differing objectives for the evening, and they had nothing to do with business.

"I'm up for some kinky things," she said to her husband. "But wife swapping isn't one of them."

"I'm telling you right now, darlin'," he whispered so just she could hear, "I'm the only one who's going to be taking that dress off you tonight."

She flushed under his gaze as memories of the past few nights came into her head. They'd knocked off Cal's remaining options from their bet, including the reverse cowgirl. At first it had been difficult for her to enjoy it, but then Cal had stroked her from her shoulders down to her waist, over her hips and across her thighs, and she'd felt how much he cared for her. The next thing she knew she'd rocked them both to completion, tossing her head back and crying out Cal's name.

Tonight it was Lucy's turn to choose an option. Just thinking about it made her nipples hard and her panties wet. Why should she be the only one who was uncomfortable?

"You know when you say things like that, cowboy, it makes me so wet."

"Jesus, darlin'. I love it when you talk like that. Makes me want to push you up against the wall, lift your skirt up, and see for myself how wet you are."

"That's exactly the option we'll be scratching off the list tonight."

He groaned and turned back to his guests. She chuckled and headed for the kitchen, making a show of checking on dinner even though she knew everything was being taken care of. After a few moments she rejoined Cal and the Gleasons in the living room with a fresh tray of hors d'oeuvres. Joel still sat on the couch, drink in hand. His wife stood next to Cal at the bar as he fixed a drink. She leaned forward, and her breasts practically fell out of her dress and onto Cal's arm.

"Come sit next to me," Joel said, patting the couch.

Lucy sat and held out the tray to him. "Would you care for an appetizer?"

"Thank you." He chose one and popped it into his mouth. "Delicious. Now you."

Before Lucy realized what he meant to do, he was pushing a Brie and crabmeat puffed pastry into her mouth. She was still chewing when he reached out and brushed his thumb across her lips.

"A crumb," he said and then licked his thumb.

Lucy swung her panicked gaze toward her husband, but he was busy making another cocktail with Anne pressed up against him as though she was interested in learning how it was done. Or else the whole front side of her had been superglued to Cal.

"You have a lovely home," Joel said, drawing her attention back to him.

"Thank you."

"You'll have to give me a tour after dinner. I'd love to see the upstairs."

"Oh, it looks a lot like the downstairs. Except with beds."

He put a hand on her thigh. "Then I'm sure I'll love it even more."

"We shouldn't hog all of the hors d'oeuvres." She popped up off the couch, making his hand slide away. "I should see if Anne and Cal would like some too."

"Excellent idea." He rose as well, placing a hand on her back where the cutout on her dress opened up to bare skin.

With her hands full of the tray, there was nothing she could do except put up with it as they made their way across the room. A sick knot twisted in her belly. This man didn't seem to care if she was interested in him or not. As soon as she could, she turned so that his hand fell away, offering the tray to Cal and Anne.

"Care for an appetizer?" She could hear the strain in her voice.

Cal must have heard it too. "Darlin', why don't you put that tray down, and I'll mix you a drink." He handed Anne her cocktail, forcing her to move back or end up with her drink down the front of her dress. "Here's your Slow Comfortable Screw, Anne."

Lucy couldn't believe the woman's nerve.

Cal leaned on the bar toward her. "What can I get for you, darlin'? How about a Harvey Wallbanger? A Screaming Orgasm? I can also do a Long Slow Comfortable Screw Up Against the Wall." He winked. "But only for you."

Lucy bit the inside of her cheek to keep from smiling, then cleared her throat. "I'd love a Long Slow Comfortable Screw Up Against the Wall. But only from you."

The rest of the evening went well, Lucy thought. Anne and Joel continued to flirt with them, but after Cal's drink offering they weren't as persistent. Cal insisted on showing their daughter off to them, which brought out a different side to Anne that Lucy appreciated. They had motherhood in common if nothing else.

Cal closed the door after waving goodbye to their

guests and leaned back against it. "I think that was the most interesting dinner party I've ever attended."

"I'm not sure interesting is the word I'd use, but it was certainly the most unique."

"You know, darlin'…" he eased away from the door and came toward her, "…you really held up your end of the bargain tonight. The food was delicious. You were a gracious and generous hostess. Not to mention the fact that you look amazing in that dress." He hooked a finger into her neckline and pulled. "Every time you bent over I got to look down it."

"You and Joel. I think next time I'll wear a turtleneck."

He let go of the front of her dress, trailing his finger up to cup the back of her neck. "Did you enjoy yourself despite the rudeness of our guests?"

"I actually did. I especially enjoyed my cocktail. I don't think I've ever had a Long Slow Comfortable Screw Up Against the Wall."

He backed her up until she met the wall. "I'm feeling challenged to remedy that, darlin'."

"You already did once tonight." She brought her arms up around his neck. "I'm counting on you to do it again."

"This is a wall," he said, moving into her. "And you're up against it."

"We're in the middle of the house."

"The caterers have gone. The staff is in their quarters. We're alone and up against a wall."

"I'm not wearing any panties."

"It drives me crazy when you talk like that," he growled.

Cal put his mouth to hers, finally able to do what he'd been dying to since he came home and saw her in this dress—mess her up. Wedging his leg between hers, he changed the angle of the kiss, grinding his thigh against her. Her gasp fanned the flames inside him to the point that he struggled for control. When she went for his belt buckle, making quick work of it, he fought to keep from shoving up her skirt and driving into her without any ceremony at all.

Kissing a path down her neck, he found the zipper at the back of her dress and drew it down. The lower the zipper got, the lower the front of her dress dipped until the sleeves slipped down her arms and she pulled them free. A flick of his fingers and he had her bra hooks undone, and it too slid down her arms.

He caressed her breasts with both hands, fondling her nipples. She went wild for him, reaching for his zipper. He felt cool air and then her hands on him. He loved the way she touched him, caressing up and down. Fisting her dress in one hand, he raised her skirt. The naughty minx hadn't lied. She was bare and wet, so unbelievably wet for him. Slipping one then two fingers into her, he groaned at how wet she was for him. She widened her legs, her head tilting back to give him access.

He nipped and kissed her neck, which he knew drove her mad. She thrust her hips against his hand, clutching at him and moaning as she drew closer to climax. He wanted to be with inside her when she came. If she kept stroking him like that it would be over before they got started. He reached a hand into his front pocket and came up with a condom, which he handed to her. She ripped open the packet with her teeth. So damn sexy when she took charge. Rolling the condom on him, she drove him insane, stroking him non stop.

He shoved her skirt all the way up, gripped her ass in both hands, and lifted her up against the wall.

Pinning her with his body, he grabbed his dick and found her entrance. He thrust up as he brought her down until he completely impaled her. God the feel of her.

He began to move in sharp, deep thrusts. She threw her head back and gasped. He knew she was close, but not as close as he was, so he slipped a hand between them and rubbed her clit. She went off, digging her nails into his shoulders. He followed her, burying himself inside her.

Dropping his forehead onto her shoulder, he struggled to regain his breath and keep them from sliding down the wall to the floor. She'd wrapped her legs around his waist, sifting a hand through his hair as she liked to do.

"And that, darlin', is a long slow comfortable screw up against the wall."

"Mmm, it's also option number fifteen. Very sly of you to put a condom in your pocket."

"Very sly of you to not wear any panties. When did you take them off?"

"Right after dinner. When did you get the condom?"

"When I went to get Poppy."

"How smart we are."

"I don't know about smart, darlin'. More like horny. Ever since your dirty talk about being wet, I've been semi-hard all night. Through cocktails, dinner, and dessert all I could think about was this." He kissed the curve of her neck. "And lifting your skirt up. Have I told you how much I love that you hardly ever wear pants?"

"I can wear skirts around you."

Jesus. When she said shit like that, it stabbed him right in the chest.

"Maybe I'll take to going without panties too," she added.

"In that case you're going to find your skirt up around your waist a lot."

Her laugh was the most magical thing he'd ever heard. She was laughing more often these days than she had when they'd first gotten married.

He reluctantly pulled out of her. She unwound her legs, and he eased her down until her feet hit the floor. She looked thoroughly ravaged and so damn sexy he wished he had another condom so he could put her back up against the wall and go for round two.

"I'll be right back, darlin'. Why don't you go on upstairs and put that dress back on."

"But we're going to bed."

"But not to sleep. That dress had me tied up in knots all evening. I'm not done with it yet."

3

"Relax your shoulders," the instructor at the shooting range told Lucy.

Lucy had finished her gun-safety class and was much more comfortable with a firearm in her hand than she'd been when she'd begun the class. The sound of it firing didn't make her flinch as much as it had when she'd first started coming to the range. She'd even managed to land most of her shots on the target. She glanced down the range at Cal, who was too busy concentrating on his target to notice her watching him. He'd shot guns since he was a kid, so he was a lot more at ease than she was.

"Good," the instructor said. "Now widen your stance a little. That's good. Go ahead."

Lucy sighted down the barrel, focusing on the target. This time she imagined it was Kevin trying to take Poppy from her. She fired. Then again, until the gun clicked empty.

She pulled her headphones off.

"That was good. More aggressive. I'm afraid to ask whose face you saw on the target," the instructor said as he recalled the target from the back of the range.

"My ex."

"I have one of those." He grinned at her. "Her face sometimes appears on my targets too." He pulled the target down and handed it to her. "Nice job. You're improving, but I'd still like to see you get in some more practice."

Most of her shots had hit the paper, and a few had torn holes through the target body. She *was* getting better.

"Next time we should do a simulation. Shooting at the black shape of a person isn't the same as shooting an actual person. The simulation gives a more real-life kind of scenario where you have to choose who to shoot and who not to shoot."

"That sounds like a good idea."

"See you next time, Mrs. Sellers."

"Thanks, Jake."

Lucy packed up her gun as she'd been taught and put it in its case. She'd clean it when she got home. Cal was still shooting, so she went into the attached store to wait for him. She was admiring a pearl-handled gun in the display case when a man came up next to her and wrapped his hand around her forearm.

"I want my daughter," a voice growled in her ear.

Kevin.

He squeezed so hard on her arm that her knees buckled. She tried to twist away, but he countered her move so that she ended up hurting herself more.

"If I have to kill you to get her, I will."

"That's the only way you'll get her."

She swung her gun case and caught him in the side of the head. He stumbled, releasing his grip on her. She tried to swing it again, but he blocked it then grabbed her arm before she could bring it around a second time.

He hauled her up and got right in her face. "You fucking cunt. You'll pay for that."

He shook her, then released her so suddenly she had to grab the display case with both hands to keep from going down. Her gun case clattered to the floor. When she turned, Kevin was gone.

"Are you all right?" A woman helped her stand. "I can't believe he came at you like that. Somebody call the police."

"I'm okay."

"Are you sure, ma'am?" one of the store employees asked.

"I saw the whole thing," the woman told the clerk.

Another employee, this one a young man, came over. "He drove off, but I got part of the license plate."

"The cops are on their way," another man said.

"I'm okay, really," Lucy tried to reassure them.

"Come and sit down, miss." The older employee took her by the elbow and directed her to a chair at the end of the counter. "You're looking kind of pale."

A little group formed around them.

"What's going on?" She heard Cal before she saw him.

"This lady was attacked right here in the store," a man told Cal.

Cal elbowed his way into the group.

"Nothing—" Lucy started.

"This man came out of nowhere," the woman interrupted. "He grabbed her, but she swung her case and got him right upside the head. And then he shook her and knocked her over."

"Then he ran out," the young store clerk filled in. "I got part of his license plate." He nodded like he was proud of what he'd done. "And Bud called the police. They're on their way."

Cal knelt next to his wife. "Lucy?"

"It was Kevin." She tried to suppress the shudders that went through her. "He threatened to take Poppy."

"You hit him?" Cal asked her.

"Yeah," Lucy said. "I surprised him. I hit him before he could hit me. " The realization of that washed through her. She'd struck back. She'd swung her case without thinking and hit him in the head. She'd always been too terrified of him to lash out. The retribution would've been too great. But this time, *this time* she'd surprised him and went after him. She hadn't let him get away with hurting her.

"Good for you." Cal took her hand in his, still kneeling at her side. "I hope that asshole has a bitch of a headache because of you."

Cal seemed proud of her, but she couldn't see past being Kevin's victim yet again. She hadn't done much more than scare him off. If only she'd had her gun out...

Sirens screamed in the distance, coming closer. She'd screwed up things for Cal. The media would get wind of this like they had the incident at their home. So far Cal was getting the bum end of this bargain they'd struck. He was supposed to be cultivating the reputation of a family man. Instead his personal life drew the worst kind of publicity. The gossip hounds had been all over their first run-in with the police. This would only make matters worse.

She shot up out of her chair. "Let's go."

"Darlin', we need to document this."

"No. Let's go home. I want to see Poppy."

"But the police are already here, ma'am," the store clerk said.

Cal pulled out his cell phone. "I'll call Sam to let him know what happened and to make sure she's okay."

"All right."

The police came in and took statements from the witnesses. The security camera had caught the whole thing on tape. By the time they were finished with the police it was nearly dark.

Lucy stared out the window as Cal drove them home. One of the smaller local newspapers had sent a photographer and reporter to the gun store and had gotten the scoop of the month when they found out that billionaire Cal Sellers and his wife had been involved in what had happened. Their photos were probably already up on the Internet. Just what Cal needed—another scandal.

"Are you all right, darlin'?"

"I'm fine."

"I know you better than that. What's going on inside that pretty little head of yours?"

She really didn't want to point out what a bad bargain he'd struck when he'd asked her to marry him, but it was true. If he was smart, he'd divorce her and marry someone without all of her baggage and drama. She'd let him visit Poppy. Cal and his daughter grew closer every day, and the fact was she loved seeing them together. Poppy deserved a daddy, and Cal was the most devoted she'd ever seen. She could never separate them now.

"If you want to divorce me, I wouldn't fight you. We could work out a schedule for Poppy. I won't ask for anything from you. I'd just need a little money to find a place and get settled. I'd pay you back every penny. The sooner the bet—"

Cal jerked the steering wheel to pull over and slammed on the brakes. He shoved the car into park and turned in his seat to look at her.

"Our deal was for one year, Lucy. One year. That's the bargain you struck. I've kept up my end of the deal, why aren't you willing to keep up yours?"

"That's the thing. I'm not keeping up my end of the deal. It's not fair to you that your wife lands you on the five o'clock news. That wasn't part of our bargain. You wanted a wife so you could present yourself as a stable family man, not a wife who regularly has brushes with her ex that require police presence." She swiped at the tears that fell, hating herself even more for bringing so much drama to the situation. "I'm an embarrassment to you, not an asset. I struck the bargain with you, thinking I could hold up my end. I'm not. And I'm sorry."

"From where I'm sitting you're more than holding up your end of our bargain." He took her face in his hands and smoothed his thumbs across her cheeks to dry her tears. "I hate that you blame yourself for what Kevin does. You're not to blame any more than Poppy is. It cuts me in two sitting here watching you cry over that asshole. He's not worth it."

"As long as Kevin keeps coming around, I'm a liability to you, not an asset."

"When I add up all of my assets, I count you and Poppy as the most valuable. Now dry your eyes and let's go home to our daughter. And I don't want to hear any more talk about divorce and liabilities."

He kissed her forehead, then put the car in gear and

pulled back onto the road. He'd said pretty much what she'd expected him to say, but she couldn't help the feeling that he didn't quite believe everything he'd told her. She knew he didn't like all the negative publicity. It had already begun to affect his business. She'd heard about the contract he didn't get and at least one investor had backed out of another project.

He said he didn't regret their marriage. She was sure there were things about it he didn't regret, but she was sure there were other things he did. Like the fact that she still didn't share his bedroom even while she welcomed him into her bed. Every night he knocked on her bedroom door and asked to be allowed in. She'd told him he didn't have to anymore, but he'd just shaken his head and insisted that he did and he would until he knew she trusted him.

Another way she was letting him down. He was right. She didn't completely trust him. She was beginning to wonder if she ever would fully trust anyone ever again. And when their year was up, would he decide that it was more trouble than it was worth to keep asking his wife for permission to sleep with her? If the press ever got wind of their unusual arrangement, what would that do to his reputation?

She grew as frustrated with herself as she knew he had to be. It seemed as though every step forward led to two back. He denied she was damaging his business as he dried her tears, but she didn't believe him. It was one more way in which they lied to each other. Everything was okay. They were working through her issues. Things were getting better.

Only they weren't.

Yeah, the sex was great, but was it enough? How much

longer before he got tired of carrying the burden of their marriage? How much longer before he got tired of begging her to be a real wife to him? And how much longer before he decided he was done with their marriage, done with her?

4

Cal hung up the phone and cursed a blue streak so broad he was sure his momma heard it all the way across the state. Another investor out. At this rate the project wouldn't start on time. He was down two investors and barely managing damage control with the others. It seemed they were fine with him when he was the playboy businessman who generated scandalous headlines, but not with a man who'd had a secret baby and then hastily married the child's mother who was being victimized by her ex.

The press had dug through Lucy's past, and soon it would come out that she'd married a man who was already married, who'd beaten her and was still harassing her months after she'd left him and married yet another man—Cal. It was one thing, apparently, to leave a string of mistresses in your wake and another to let a woman with a sordid past drop a baby on your doorstep and coerce you into marrying her. At least that was how the press was spinning it.

His publicist, Charity, had been wearing holes in the

carpet in front of his desk most of the day, strategizing with him on how they were going to contain this mess and maintain his reputation for being a sharp-minded businessman who didn't put up with anyone's bullshit. More than once he'd caught her looking at him from under her lashes, no doubt wondering like everyone else how a woman like Lucy had gotten her hooks into him when every socialite in Texas hadn't been able to snare him.

The whole thing pissed him off to no end. Lucy was his wife. Poppy was his daughter. He was taking care of his responsibilities and building a life with the woman he loved. And damn it all if he didn't love her so much he could hardly catch his breath sometimes. She scared the shit out of him at the same time as she made him gladder than any man had a right to be. He looked forward to going home at the end of the day and hated to leave at the beginning.

He didn't give two shits what anyone else thought of him, but it killed him what they were saying about Lucy. More importantly, it would kill her to know what they were saying. She was smart enough to have picked up that he was having business problems and considered herself a liability to him. When she'd offered divorce in the car the other day, he'd about lost his shit. The last thing he wanted was a divorce. They'd find a way to work through this.

That bastard Walker would be caught, and the publicity surrounding them would die down, and everything would go back to normal. Or at least a semblance of normalcy. Lucy moving her things into the master bedroom had become a symbol to him of them having a real marriage. Instead he still visited her every night like a boyfriend, coming across the hall and knocking on her door for a sleepover. Not that he was complaining. Hell no.

They'd come miles from where they'd started. And while there were still times when she'd panic and make him stop or pull out, there were other times when he glimpsed the old Lucy. His Lucy. In those moments she'd drop her head back and enjoy what they did together. Uninhibited and wild, letting her intense sexuality free, was when she was the real Lucy. He'd come to live for those moments and tried to invent new ways to make them come out.

They were building something unexpected and necessary together, and he hated the thought that people on the outside would try to tear it down before they'd gotten a chance to explore it. And he hated that he was going to have to ask Lucy to go in front of a camera to tell her side of the story. His publicist, Charity, had thought she'd be great in an interview with her girl-next-door looks and his baby on her hip. They'd film it at their home to really highlight the family-man image Cal needed to show the public to rebuild his reputation.

He glanced down at the script on the desk in front of him. Lucy would have to memorize her part to make sure she stayed on message, Charity had said. And to make sure she didn't ad-lib something they didn't want broadcasted. When he'd proposed marriage to Lucy, he had no idea he'd be asking her to do more than the occasional dinner party or charity event. He certainly hadn't expected her to be the key to potentially saving Sellers Investments.

His reservations about having her do this interview ran as deep as his need for her to do it. She was still so fragile. He worried what the pressure of it would do to her. Charity and the board might not like it, but if Lucy said no to the interview, then she wouldn't do it. Consequences be damned.

"What about this one?" Charity held up a matching blue blouse and skirt. The color reminded him of Lucy's eyes.

"I like it. And that pink set too."

Charity had had his assistant, Felicia, pick up several outfits for Lucy to try on and decide which she was more comfortable in for the interview. He was relieved to see that there was no frilly fifties-style apron or string of pearls to really drive home the wife-and-mother point.

"What have you got for the ball?" he asked.

Charity showed him a half-dozen dresses. In the end he told her to send them all to the house for Lucy to select one for the annual Dallas Young Professionals Ball. Cal was set to give the keynote speech this year. As his wife she was expected to attend and be properly dressed. He'd already purchased a sapphire-and-diamond necklace and earring set that matched her engagement ring for her to wear at the event and instructed Charity to choose dresses that would go with them.

He only hoped Lucy wouldn't think all this work had been done for her because she couldn't be trusted to turn up in something appropriate. Who was he kidding? That was *exactly* why all this work had been done on her behalf. His publicist wanted Lucy to wear a dress that would be—in her words—flattering, yet modest, appropriate, yet cutting edge, tasteful, yet elegant. Whatever all that bull meant. All he really wanted was for Lucy to look and feel beautiful. And if the dress showed a lot of cleavage, he'd be extra happy, but he had a feeling that tasteful meant a lack of exposed skin.

As soon as Charity left he gathered up his things, anxious to see his wife and daughter. Felicia knocked and then entered the room, shutting the door behind her.

"What is it, Felicia?" Cal asked.

"I know you're about to head home, but Mrs. Gleason is here. She says it's urgent."

He snapped his briefcase closed and set it next to his desk. "Send her in."

He finished setting his desk to rights as Felicia went to get Anne Gleason. He wondered what could be so all-fired important that she needed to see him at six o'clock in the evening without her husband. This couldn't be good.

Anne swept into the room, wearing one of those dresses that tied around the neck and pushed a woman's breasts up to her chin. He had to give it to her, she had nice tits, but they didn't hold a candle to Lucy's. Still he looked. He was a guy after all, and she'd put them out there to be looked at.

"Cal, darling. Thank you for seeing me without an appointment."

She hit him with her whole body, wrapping her arms around his neck and giving him a full-on kiss on the lips. Behind her he saw Felicia's scowl before she shut the door. Shit.

He unwound Anne's arms and pushed her back. "What can I do for you, Mrs. Gleason?"

She had the nerve to pout as she stroked the lapel of his suit jacket. "Now, Cal, I thought we were friends. When you call me Mrs. Gleason, it makes me think of my mother-in-law, and she was an awful bitch. Call me Anne."

He pulled her hand off him and gestured for her to

have a seat in one of the chairs on the other side of his desk. "Please have a seat...Anne."

Instead of doing what he wanted her to do, she propped her hip on top of his desk and leaned forward so he had a clear view down the front of her dress. She wasn't wearing a bra.

"I'm so glad you could see me. I wanted to thank you again for the lovely dinner at your house," she said.

"Your thanks belong to Lucy. She did all the work. I'll be sure to pass them along to her again."

"Joel was quite taken with her. It was Lucy this and Lucy that all the way home. He's become a bit obsessed. So I've come to invite you to dinner in our home. Just the two of you. We've got a wonderful wine cellar, so you might want to plan for an overnight stay so you can thoroughly enjoy yourself."

"I'll arrange for a driver that evening. What night are we talking about?"

"Oh, the sooner the better. How about this Friday, say around seven? Dress casually. I'm thinking of having Indian food. We'll sit on pillows on the floor. It will all be very decadent and intimate."

Lucy was going to hate spending another evening with the Gleasons, especially in a setting they couldn't control. But he really couldn't afford to say no. Buying Joel Gleason's company would give him what he needed to not have to depend on investors for future projects. And he was looking forward to the day when he wouldn't have to deal with investors.

"Let me check with Lucy to make sure we don't already have plans, and get back to you."

She clapped her hands together. "Lovely. I hope you can make it. I have something *very special* in mind for us."

She winked and hopped off his desk, making her breasts jiggle. Before he could stop her, she planted another kiss on his lips, then walked out the door with a wiggle of her ass.

He wiped his mouth with the back of his hand, then rubbed off her lipstick with one of the hand-stitched handkerchiefs Lucy had made him. If the way Anne behaved was any indication, they were going to be spending the evening getting backed into corners and swatting away hands. There was no way he was going to subject Lucy to that. He'd have to find another way to persuade Joel to sell him his company.

LUCY STARED at the gorgeous clothes scattered across her bed and hanging from the back of the closet doors. There was no note, just a comment from their housekeeper Hazel about how they were for her from Cal. Six evening gowns with matching shoes and bags and four different skirt-and-blouse combinations with accessories. What could they be for? She'd already bought what she thought was a nice dress for the Dallas Young Professionals Ball next week. Did he not trust her judgment?

She hadn't spent as much on her dress as these dresses must have cost, but hers was still nice. And it fit. Fitting had been an issue in the dressing room and the reason she hadn't bought the dress she'd really wanted. That and the money. She couldn't bring herself to pay more than she would've if she'd been using her own money instead of Cal's. It just didn't feel right to her.

There was a knock on her bedroom door. She opened it to find Cal filling up the doorway. Her body reacted before her mind could with a stuttering in her chest followed by a flush that brought a tightening of her nipples and a wetness between her legs. If he threw her on the bed right now, she'd be ready to take him. It was as though her body recognized him as her mate and prepared itself for him. She'd never felt this with any other man except Cal. It both frightened and thrilled her.

"Hello, darlin'." He leaned down and kissed her cheek.

She loved how he called her darlin' with that long, slow drawl of his like a long, slow, full-body caress. Heat flashed through her again, and she was sure her cheeks were as pink as her blouse.

"Hey there, cowboy. How was your day?"

"Better now that I'm home. Can I come in?"

She opened the door wider, inviting him in. She loved how he asked her permission, putting her in control. He'd said he liked it and that it kept him honest, but she had a suspicion he wasn't confident he'd get a yes every time. That had to be the most attractive thing about this new Cal. This man who was her husband and lover had given her the gift to heal at great personal risk.

"Ah." He shoved his hands in his pockets and rocked back on his heels, surveying the clothes scattered across the bedroom. "I see the delivery arrived."

"I'm assuming there's a reason you did this."

"It wasn't so much me as my publicist, Charity. She seems to feel that the right clothes make the right impression."

"I see. So until now I've been making the wrong impression?"

He pulled his hands out of his pockets and held them palms up. "No, darlin', not at all. That isn't why these clothes are here."

"So why are they here?"

"The dresses are for the ball. Charity says that as my wife you have to look the part, especially now with the negative publicity because of your asshole ex."

"I already bought a dress though."

"Sorry. I didn't know that." He walked over and examined three of the dresses that hung from the back of one of the closet doors. "I did have one requirement that it looks like Charity somehow managed to fulfill."

She crossed her arms over her chest, feeling insecure about this Charity fulfilling any of Cal's *requests*. "What was that?"

He pulled a long, thin, lidded box from the inside pocket of his suit jacket and held it out to her. "They had to go with these." When she didn't immediately take it, he extended it out farther. "Go on. Open it."

She accepted the box, frowning over the expensive gold lettering from an upscale jeweler downtown. "What is it?"

"Open it."

"It's not my birthday."

"I know."

She pulled the ribbon off and lifted the lid. Nestled inside was a fine filigree pendant with pearls, sapphires, and diamonds on a long, thin chain and a pair of earrings that perfectly matched. She couldn't stop staring at them, tracing a finger over the intricate design that matched the engagement ring he'd given her. It was too extravagant and too expensive for someone like her, but she loved it. She absolutely loved it.

"Do you like them?"

She'd almost forgotten he was in the room. She'd been so taken with the beauty and intricacy of the design and the thought that something as beautiful as these could belong to her.

"They match your ring, except that I had pearls added. They're Poppy's birthstone."

He sounded nervous. She glanced up to find him watching her with a look so intense her breath caught. He expected her to reject them, to reject him.

"I know," she said. "They're absolutely beautiful. But why?"

He let out a breath as if he'd been holding it waiting for her answer. "I wanted you to have something pretty."

"These aren't pretty, they're absolutely gorgeous."

His mouth curved up into a smile as his confidence fully returned. "I'm glad you like them." He lifted her left hand. "I know colored stones aren't what's fashionable, but the sapphires reminded me of your eyes."

Damn it! When he said things like that, it made her eyes all watery.

"Hey, are you crying?" He pulled his handkerchief from his pocket and handed it to her. "Are those happy tears?"

She nodded and sniffed, dabbing at the corners of her eyes with his handkerchief. "You always know what to say to make me turn into a watering pot."

"Come here, darlin'." He took her into his arms and rubbed her back. "I'm glad you like the jewelry. That's stressful stuff for a man."

"I like how you included Poppy in it." She sniffed back more tears. "I'm sorry I didn't tell you when I was pregnant with her. I'm sorry you weren't there when she was born and for all the months since. You're a really good father."

"Aww, Jesus, darlin', when you talk like that... I didn't

deserve to be a father to her, but now I think I might. I'm trying real hard, and the truth of it is, she's the best thing I've ever done, however accidentally and messed up I did it. I'm glad I've got this chance with her and with you."

"Me too."

She pulled back enough so she could go up on her toes and kiss him. As with everything with Cal, things got out of hand quickly, and before she knew it he'd backed her up against the dresses on the closet door with a knee between her legs, one hand on her breast and the other lifting up her skirt. Poppy started crying, and his hands fell away.

He put his forehead to hers and let out a breath. "Damn, darlin', you've get me going from zero to sixty in about two seconds." He kissed her hard on the mouth. "I'll go get her." He left to tend to his daughter.

She'd grown accustomed to having a real parenting partner since their marriage. Poppy lit up around her daddy. It was a treasure to watch the two of them together. She was starting to think that maybe things could work out for them. And that got her tearing up again. She unfolded Cal's handkerchief to dry her eyes and froze. Lipstick. Red lipstick on the handkerchief she'd hand embroidered and had given to him. And he'd used it to wipe lipstick off. Off of what? And whose lipstick was it?

"Here she is." Cal came into the room holding Poppy. "Sam said she heard my voice and started crying for me."

He turned his face and kissed their daughter, and she saw the smudge of red at the side of his mouth. Her heart kicked out a ragged beat, and she flushed for an entirely different reason. This was how it had started the first time. Little signs that Lucy had ignored or made excuses for. In the end all of her denial couldn't excuse the secretary Cal had bent over his desk and almost screwed. Hell, maybe he already had, and that scene in his office was one of many times he'd cheated on her. She only had his word to go by, and she wasn't sure how good that word really was.

Now he was back at it. She'd been right not to trust him. Her mother had trusted her daddy even when he came home reeking of perfume with love bites on his neck. The last thing Lucy wanted for herself or for Poppy was a recreation of her childhood. Poppy would never hide in her room while her father fucked another woman as soon as her mother left the house. And she sure as hell didn't want to ever look the other way like her mother did.

She reached up, swiped the lipstick off with her thumb and showed it to him along with the stained handkerchief. "Looks like you didn't get rid of all the evidence. You're getting sloppy."

5

"Oh, that." He chuckled. "Anne Gleason stopped by my office to invite us to dinner."

"And you kissed her."

"*She* kissed *me*." He narrowed his eyes at her. "What are you implying?"

"It's not like there's no history here."

"We're not having this out in front of our daughter."

He left the room. Lucy stewed like an overfilled pressure cooker. She didn't have the self-confidence she'd had the first time she'd caught Cal cheating, but what she did have was a limit for how long she'd listen to him stammer and make excuses as to why he fell face first into another woman's cleavage. Or why he couldn't seem to keep his lips off another woman's lips.

He came back and closed the door behind him. "You're right. There is a history here, but it's ancient history. I'm not cheating on you."

"Yet? Or not at all?"

"Not at all."

"What am I supposed to think when I find this?" She

shook the lipstick-stained handkerchief at him. "How would you feel if you found evidence that I'd been with another man? How would you feel if you *walked in* on me with another man?"

"Before or after I punched him in the face?"

"I told you when we started this that I couldn't take you cheating on me again."

"I'm not. I wouldn't."

She stared at him, trying to find the truth in his expression. He hadn't gotten to where he was without perfecting his poker face. But he wasn't doing it this time. He stared straight back at her, and she could see the regret mixed in with something else—desperation. He not only wanted her to trust him, he needed her to. Her eyes teared up for a whole other reason.

She started to dab at her eyes with the stained handkerchief, then pulled the gesture in disgust and threw it on the ground. "I believe you."

He sagged in visible relief. "It's the truth, darlin'. I haven't touched another woman since you stormed out of my office and out of my life. Every time I started to think I could be with someone else, thoughts of you would pop into my head, and everything in me would freeze up. No matter how many women I dated after we split up, none of them were you. None of them tossed their hair over their shoulder and jutted out a hip like you do. None of them made me feel both humble and like a conquering hero like you do. And I knew if I took them to bed that none of them would make that sound you make when I first thrust inside you.

"Or make me come so hard I think I might just die from it. And none of them would ever make me want to drop to my knees and beg to be believed. Because if you don't believe me, we're over. And I can't be without you again, Lucy. I just can't. So I'm thanking God you believe me. And I'm thanking you for giving me this second chance with you."

She was sobbing now, covering her face with both hands, as he dropped to his knees and wrapped his arms around her waist.

"I won't screw this up. I won't."

She cradled his head against her chest and cried harder. She was right to trust in him. She knew how aggressive Anne Gleason was toward Cal and how she hadn't hid her desire to sleep with him. His words played over and over in her head. He hadn't been with another woman since they'd split up? She could hardly wrap her mind around it. He'd gone without for seventeen months while she'd given herself to someone who had ruined her life and was still ruining it.

She cried for the time they'd lost together and the mistakes they'd made and for the sheer joy of finding each other again after all they'd been through. She couldn't seem to stop crying until Cal lifted his head to look up at her and she bent to kiss him. The rising tide of sorrow and regret inside her spilled over, catching fire and morphing into something else altogether.

And then she was kissing him for an entirely different reason that had nothing to do with the past and everything to do with the future, their future together. She dropped to her knees in front of him, yanking on his shirt, desperate for the feel of him under her hands. She managed the first couple of buttons and then just pulled the whole thing over his head. Her blouse hit the floor next to his shirt.

Cal let her have her way, shoving at his clothes, then

hers. She believed him. When he'd never given her any reason to in the past. He'd lied back then and hid things from her and offered up the worst kind of betrayal. And she'd taken him back, taken him into her bed and her heart again. It was all he could think about as he laid her down on and crawled between her wide-spread legs, as he rolled the condom on and lowered himself over her.

He entered her slowly, watching her face and the way she dropped her head back and arched into his entry. He thrust hard into her just to hear the sound she made when he was fully seated. God he loved her. He pulled back and then came at her again a little harder, and then again and again, building the pressure between them until he was sweating from the effort and she was crying out so loud he was sure the whole house heard her.

When he finally let loose, rocking deep into her, it did feel like he might die. There was no other moment more perfect than being inside Lucy. He'd live inside her if he could.

Her hot breath blew on his cheek as he lay on top of her. He knew she was looking at him, but he couldn't quite meet her gaze yet. The rawness of being inside her, of pressing himself into her, was still too new. He needed another moment before he could look into her eyes without tearing his heart out of his chest and laying it at her feet.

When he had control again, he turned his head to look at her. Her face was pink, her full lips were red, and her tear-filled eyes were so blue they rivaled a winter sky.

"I won't screw this up," he told her, his voice as scraped out as he was.

"I know." She smiled at him even as the last tear slid down her cheek and into her hair. "Will you help me move my things across the hall? I want to sleep with my husband in our bed. Tonight."

CAL LAY in bed that night, listening to his wife wash her face and brush her teeth in the bathroom, feeling like the luckiest man in the world. She trusted him. She finally trusted him. Ironically it had taken another woman's lipstick on him to do it. No more walking across the hall to knock on her door and the sickening feeling low in his stomach at the thought that she might not let him in. But now, now he didn't have to worry.

They'd spent the rest of the evening moving her things and then played with their daughter on the big bed before reading her a story and putting her to sleep for the night. It had felt real and right. They were a family in every sense of the word. He stacked his hands under his head and stared up at the ceiling he hadn't seen in weeks, not exactly sure how he'd accomplished it.

Lucy came out of the bathroom dressed in some kind of flimsy see-through thing that had him sitting up in bed so he could get a better look. She wasn't wearing a damn thing underneath.

"What do you think?" She spun for him, and the fabric flew out around her.

He had trouble forming any thoughts except for ones he couldn't repeat. It was like someone had wrapped all of his favorite things in gauze so that he couldn't quite see them.

"It was a gift from Mi." She held the dress out at the sides, looking a little unsure. "I was supposed to wear it for our wedding night."

"We can pretend tonight's our wedding night."

"But do you like it?"

"It's a tease. Come here and let me rip it off you."

She laughed. "Don't you dare tear it. It's too beautiful."

"Then you better take it off before you climb up here, darlin', because I can't be responsible for my actions once your knee hits the mattress."

She looked down at herself, smoothing her hands over her body, and then she lifted the skirt and pulled the whole thing over her head. Instead of joining him, she went into the closet.

He strained to keep her fine ass in view. "Where are you going?"

"To hang it up. I don't want it ruined."

She came back out wearing nothing but the jewelry he'd given her. He decided right then and there that he'd buy her a whole shop full of jewels if she came to bed dressed just like that every night.

She climbed up next to him, which was a bit of a struggle for her. He made a note to get a step for her or else buy a whole new bed she didn't have to strain herself to get into. The only exerting he wanted her to do in bed was with him. She straddled him and flipped her hair back over her shoulders so that her breasts were fully exposed.

"I was thinking," she said, "that we could try option number two." She pulled a scarf from underneath one of the pillows and wrapped it in her fists, tugging on it to make it snap.

He ran his hands up her thighs. "Whatever that option is, I'm on board."

"It's the binding option, the one where I tie you up."

"However you want me, wherever you want me, I'm there."

She looked at the carved wooden headboard with a frown. "There's no place to tie your hands to."

"Hmm, that is a problem. What if you tied my hands together and I have to keep them above my head no matter what? And then tomorrow I'll have a new bed delivered with a step for you to climb up and a wrought-iron headboard you can tie me up to any time you like."

"That seems awfully extreme for just the one option."

While she'd been deciding what to do, his hands had wandered up her thighs to her breasts, and he rolled her nipples between his fingers. She moaned and arched her back.

"If you've got your heart dead set on that option, then there's only one thing to do—buy a new bed." He leaned up and replaced one of his hands with his mouth.

"We don't...ooohhh...need a new bed." She fell forward, catching herself with one hand on the head-board, giving him better access.

He could've spent all night on her breasts. They were so sensitive that one touch had her rubbing herself against him. He could feel her slickness, smell her heat as she moved. He barely touched her, and yet she was so ready for him. He drifted a hand down her back to her ass and slipped a finger into her from behind. She moved up and down, pleasuring herself on his hand. With his other hand he slid a finger in from the front. She went wild then, bucking up and down. He added two more fingers, and she groaned, her breasts jiggling with her move-ments. He leaned up and caught her nipple between his lips and sucked hard.

She came on a long, low moan, her head back, lips

parted, her hair a wild mess around her. He released her nipple and laid back to watch as her orgasm rolled through her. She was so goddamned beautiful he could hardly believe she was his.

She collapsed onto his chest as her orgasm faded. "I'm never, ever going to tie your hands up. They're too good. That thing you just did with them. Oh, my God."

"I don't know about that. That no-hands option we tried a while back was pretty damn great."

"This was better."

"I'm not done with you yet, Mrs. Sellers. This is our wedding night." He rolled them so that he was on top. "We have to consummate our marriage to make it legal and binding."

"Mmm, binding."

He adjusted the pendant he'd given her so that it fell between her breasts. "We'll get to the binding. But first I want to make love to my wife. This would be option number thirty-seven."

She ran her hands into his hair. "And what happens in this option?"

"This is the option where I ruin you for all other men."

"That might have already happened about three minutes ago."

"That was nothing. Just an appetizer."

He kissed her as he'd wanted to on their wedding day, sealing their vows. And then changed it, kissing her deep and long. Running a hand down her body, he mapped her curves, caressing her waist as it dipped in and her hip as it flared out. Long, slow movements down then up her leg. He repeated the motion over and over, his hand skimming her inner thigh and the underside of her breast, but never giving her what she wanted.

Her hands were all over him, relearning him as he was her. He kissed a trail along her jaw and down her neck. She shifted, nestling him between her legs. He wanted to go slow, but she had her hand on his ass and her knees bent so she was wide open. She kissed him like she more than wanted him, she needed him.

He broke the kiss and looked down at her. Her eyes were so blue, bluer than the stones between her breasts, and she was smiling up at him. No hesitation, no fear, she was his Lucy once again. He bent and kissed the slope of each of her breasts, gliding his tongue in circles until he was tracing around her nipples. She held his head in her hands, making little moaning sounds. He pulled her nipples into his mouth, one and then the other. By the time he glanced up at her face, she was squirming under him.

She grabbed the condom off the nightstand and rolled it on, taking her time about it. He'd get her back for that. While she was busy torturing him, he slid two fingers into her. She sucked in a breath. He gently stroked her clit, easing her legs wider apart. He kissed her, mimicking the thrusts of his hand. She clutched at him, and he knew she was close so he slowed down.

This wasn't going to be one of their mad couplings. He wanted to show her with his body what he felt for her and how she made him feel when he was with her, inside her. She gripped his ass and tilted her hips, trying to get him to hurry it along, but he kept up the slow, agonizing pace until he felt her give over to it. Her head dropped back, exposing her neck for him to kiss, so he obliged her.

He positioned himself at her entrance, and for a brief moment he hesitated. And then he saw his ring on her hand and everything they were, everything they would be, slid into place for him.

"Look at me," he told her.

Her lashes fluttered open. Their gazes locked as he eased into her. When he hit deep, she made that sound that drove him mad, and he nearly lost it. He had to take several breaths to hold on to some kind of control. And then he pulled back and slid into her again. Stroking in and out, he kept the pace where he wanted it, but not quite where she needed it. He watched her expression change as she drew close to coming.

"I want you to look at me. I'm the one inside you." He drove into her harder, watching as her lips parted and she drew nearer to orgasm. "I'm your husband." He pumped faster into her, and she bit her lip, digging her nails into his back. "And I love you."

She sucked in a breath and came, still biting her lip. He thrust into her once more, jerking as he too found release and collapsed on top of her. This time he faced her, waiting for her to turn her head and look at him.

She finally did, her gaze roaming over his face as if seeing him for the first time.

"I love you too," she whispered.

6

Cal proudly escorted his wife into the Dallas Young Professionals Ball. The ballroom had been decorated in an under-the-sea theme. Blue-green lighting made it feel as if they were underwater. They weaved around seaweed that sprang up from the floor along with anemones and other sea life. Decorative fish hung from the ceiling, and the fabric on the walls seemed to wave as if affected by a current.

Lucy had chosen a royal-blue floor-length dress that tucked in at the waist and showed a reasonable amount of cleavage. It was his favorite of all the dresses Felicia had dropped off for Lucy to choose from. Lucy's hair was piled up on her head, exposing her creamy white skin and the necklace and earrings he'd given her. She was by far the most beautiful woman in the room. He couldn't take his eyes off her. A lot of other men couldn't either, he noticed.

Lucas had arranged for them to have bodyguards disguised as guests. One male and one female, so that when Lucy went anywhere—even to the ladies' room— she was never alone. Cal wasn't about to take another chance that her bastard ex could get to her. Poppy was at home, well protected by Sam and the security team that regularly patrolled the grounds of their estate as well as in-house staff whose sole purpose was to protect one tiny redheaded little girl.

Cal scanned the room and nearly groaned out loud when he spotted Joel and Anne Gleason headed their way.

He leaned down to whisper in Lucy's ear. "If either of them offers you a drink, don't take it. I wouldn't put it past them to roofie us."

Lucy glanced sharply up at him. "They wouldn't."

"You want to take that chance, darlin'? The only thing we drink tonight we get from the bar ourselves."

"Cal, Lucy, how wonderful to see you," Anne said.

She air-kissed Lucy and tried to go for Cal's lips, but he successfully dodged her and planted a kiss on her cheek instead. He shook hands with Joel and watched very closely how he greeted Lucy. Joel gave her a chaste kiss on the cheek, but his gaze was glued to her chest.

Lucy tried to hide her revulsion for the Gleasons, especially after Anne had attempted to kiss Cal on the mouth. Again. She didn't consider herself a violent person, but she'd have no problem pulling her gun from her purse, hoping Anne would get the point that Cal was hers.

"I never did hear back from you about dinner," Anne was saying. "We'd love to have the two of you over. What about the weekend after next? Do you have plans?"

"A friend of mine owns Sur La Mer downtown. I could get us a table," Cal offered.

Anne waved away his suggestion. "No restaurants. I insist on returning the hospitality."

"I've just acquired a case of Château d'Yquem," Joel said. "We haven't had an occasion to open it yet. Don't disappoint my wife. She loves to play hostess."

Joel couldn't have laid down the ultimatum any stronger. This was a hurdle she and Cal would have to jump in order to make the deal Cal needed so badly.

"We'd love to," Lucy agreed, despite her feelings for the Gleasons. She knew Cal still hadn't persuaded Joel to sell him his company. "Thank you so much for the invitation."

"It's settled then," Anne said. "Dinner at our place a week from Friday at six o'clock."

Joel rubbed his hands together, his gaze firmly fastened on Lucy's cleavage. "I've been looking forward to showing you my collection of taxidermy from all over the world, Cal. We've got a lot to discuss you and I."

Lucy wanted to ask why anyone would want to collect dead animals, but she could see that Cal was nearly at his limit for politeness.

"Oh, look. Mimi Vanderclark is waving us over," Lucy said. "I'm so sorry to have to leave you," she told the Gleasons. "But Mimi is an old family friend, and if I don't say hello, I'll never hear the end of it. Won't you excuse us?"

They said their goodbyes to the Gleasons, and Cal led them across the room where Lucy had pointed.

"Who's Mimi Vanderclark?" Cal asked.

"I made her up. I'm awful, aren't I?"

"No, you're brilliant."

They were waylaid by some business associates of Cal's, a couple of whom recognized Lucy from her days as the cohost of *Pleasure at Home*. Everyone seemed interested in speaking with her. There were a lot of questions about them and the rumors running through the media.

Cal extricated them from those situations and maneuvered them around the ballroom so that by the time they found their table, Lucy was pretty sure she'd met everyone in the room.

Cal pulled a chair out for her and waited for her to be seated before he took his seat next to her.

"Have I told you how beautiful you look tonight?"

"Only about eighty times."

"All I can think about is getting that dress off you."

"I don't know why. It's not like I'm wearing anything underneath it."

He groaned, leaned in to nip her earlobe, and proceeded to tell her exactly what he wanted to do to her once he got her dress off. By the time he finished, she was sure she'd flushed from her neckline to her forehead. She had to take several gulps of water before she felt like she had herself under control.

The MC began the program with a handful of corny jokes about businessmen, which earned him pity laughs. The awards ceremony was filled with names of people Lucy had only ever heard of or read about on TV or online. Every time one was announced, Cal would lean over and tell her something unrepeatable about them. A few times she had to cover her mouth to keep from laughing out loud and embarrassing Cal.

After that, dinner was served. It was surprisingly good for a banquet dinner. And then Cal told her how much it had cost per plate, and she knew why. Lucy was surprised to be having such a good time in a room full of people she had absolutely nothing in common with. The dinner conversation wasn't nearly as boring as she'd expected.

Cal nudged her arm to get her attention away from the woman next to her. "How do I look?"

She examined him, which wasn't a hardship. "You look great. Very handsome."

"Good. I'm on next, and they're about to announce me."

As soon as the words were out of his mouth, his name was called and he stood to a round of applause that kept going until he quieted the crowd from the podium. The audience seemed to enjoy Cal's speech, laughing at his jokes and nodding along with his observations. Lucy was so proud of her husband she could burst.

A siren pealed, interrupting Cal midsentence. A mechanical voice came over the loudspeakers, warning that this was a fire alarm and telling everyone to exit the building.

"I guess my speech was too hot," Cal joked, then motioned for Lucy to stay where she was, standing next to their table.

All of a sudden there was a lot of shouting and people rushing toward the doors. Smoke billowed from the overhead vents. Someone pushed Lucy, knocking her forward and into the swelling crowd that grew more frantic to get through the only open exit at the back of the room. She struggled to stay on her feet, but as the air got thicker, hits came from every side. She glanced back at the podium, hoping to catch sight of Cal, but he was gone.

A lick of fear slithered up her spine. Where was he? She'd worked her way out of the funnel of the crowd and out into the fringes of the room. Alone. She looked around for the two bodyguards Cal had hired, but they were nowhere in sight.

A hand grabbed her arm, yanking her back against a hard form. "Remember..." Kevin's harsh murmur in her ear sent her heart skidding, "...I can get to you anywhere.

Any time." He released her, shoving her back into the mass of people, hurdling her closer to the exit.

She pushed blindly into the swell, knocking into people to get away. By the time she reached the double doors that led to the hallway, panic crawled all over her like biting ants. She had to get to Poppy. She had to make sure her daughter was safe.

Cal caught up to her just as she reached the street door. He wrapped an arm around her waist, pulling her into his side. She grasped fistfuls of his jacket, hanging on to him for more than the steadying effect he was having on her senses. He was safety. He was everything she'd come to rely on, everything she needed in this world.

"I've got you, darlin'. You're all right."

"Kevin's here. He's here."

"I saw. I can't believe the balls of that son of a bitch."

He ushered her past the fire trucks and police to their waiting limo and practically shoved her inside. As soon as he shut the door, enclosing them in the protective cocoon of the car, she grabbed for him again, climbing him to get closer.

"Hey." He held her tight, his face buried in her shoulder. "You're okay. I've got you now. It'll all be okay." The subtle tremor in his voice made a liar out of him. "He can't get you. He's not going to get you."

"He did. He does. Over and over he gets to me." She was sobbing now, beating her fists against Cal's chest. He let her. "And he'll get to Poppy too. You can't stop him. No one can stop him. He gets arrested then set free. You hire guards. He gets around them. He keeps coming." She collapsed, shaking, her voice as weak as she felt. "He just keeps coming."

Cal let Lucy have her rage. When he'd witnessed her

bastard ex grab her, he'd leapt over a table to get to her, but by the time he got there, the asshole was gone and Lucy had been in a running panic for the door. He'd caught up to her too late. Every goddamned time he was too late. She was right. Walker kept coming and would probably keep coming after Lucy and Poppy until someone stopped him. Or put a bullet in him.

He didn't know what to say to soothe her, could hardly wrap his head around the terror of seeing that bastard's hands on her and the utter helplessness of watching her break down in his lap. It was his fault. All of his damn money couldn't give Lucy the one thing she needed more than the mansion she lived in and the jewels that lay against her skin—safety. He could hire a thousand bodyguards, arm her until she buckled under the weight of the guns, and use his connections until he burned through every favor owed to him, and it still wouldn't be enough.

"I'm sorry," he offered, knowing it was no kind of consolation for what she'd been through.

"I need to see Poppy."

"We're on our way home. I'm sure she's fine. Probably sleeping."

"I need to see her. Right now."

"I'll call Sam and check in." He pulled his phone out of his pocket and hit Sam's speed-dial number. Sam picked up on the first ring. Cal put the call on speakerphone. "Hey, Sam. How's Poppy?"

"She went down like a champ."

Lucy took the phone. "I want to see her."

"Hang on," Sam said. "Let me call you right back."

Lucy stared at the phone without speaking. Cal couldn't quite get a read on her. Her emotions seemed to be all over the place. Was it any wonder with the hell her ex was putting her through?

His phone rang again. Lucy grabbed for it and answered. Sam held a finger to his lips, then turned the phone so they could see the outline of Poppy sleeping peacefully in her bed, lit by only the nightlight in her room, her breathing deep and even. Lucy let out a tense breath and ran a finger over the image of their daughter.

Then the camera was back on Sam as he made his way out into the hall. "What happened?" Sam's voice had a different tone now, all business. He must have suspected they'd run into trouble at the ball.

"I'll tell you about it when we get home. Thanks, Sam. Really," Cal said. "I mean it. Thanks."

"I'd say I was just doing my job, but making sure that little girl is safe feels more like a mission than a job. See you when you get here." Sam ended the call.

"See, darlin'. She's just fine."

"She's not fine. None of us are fine. He started that fire to get to me. What if someone was injured or killed?"

He pried the phone from her hand and threw it on the seat next to them. He cupped her face, wanting her complete attention. "Let me get something straight for you right now. Nothing that asshole does or did is your fault. Got it?"

"*All* of it is my fault. I brought him into my life. I stayed too long with him. I put our daughter in danger—"

"Damn it! Stop it!"

She stiffened, and her eyes went wide.

"Shit!"

He released her, and she crawled off his lap and as far away as she could. It took every ounce of self-control he had to stay where he was and not follow her and grab her.

The way she stared at him...like he was that bastard who'd beaten and raped her. Fuck it all! He struck the window with the side of his fist, and she flinched.

"I told you I would never hurt you." He couldn't keep the anger out of his voice. The whole thing was just so fucked up.

"I know."

He watched the way she hugged herself, rubbing her arm where Walker's hand had been, huddling in the farthest corner of the car from him. If he thought he was angry before, it was nothing compared to this new rage. The sharpness of it sliced at his control.

"When you cower from me... I can't fucking take it."

She continued to stare at him as though he would leap on top of her at any moment. The last thing she needed was to be trapped in the back of a car with an angry, out-of-control man. He grasped for some calm to smother the rage that clawed at him.

"I'm sorry."

She blinked in rapid succession, her body stiff, her lips pressed tightly together.

He took a deep breath and tried again. "You're safe here. You're safe with me." Only his tone was off. He'd ended up yelling what should've been soothing.

Her small voice came to him from across the car. "Don't shout."

"What?"

"Don't shout at me." This time stronger.

He laughed even though there was nothing funny here. The fury at what she'd been through was always there, lapping at his insides and leaving scars he didn't think would ever heal. He thought he'd learned to live with it. But there she was, still cowering like a wounded puppy, waiting for the next strike, telling him to stop his shouting, and he realized that he hadn't managed his rage at all. He'd ignored it, hoping it would go the fuck away.

Every time she'd flinch if he came at her too quickly or shrink from him if he showed an ounce of anger or impatience, he'd flush hot, infuriated for her, and at himself, her ex, the whole goddamned situation. It had gotten harder and harder to control his emotions around her until he felt like he was walking on cracking ice, staring into the abyss beneath it, expecting it to pull him under.

He let out a heavy sigh. "I'm trying."

"Try harder." Her chin came up a fraction of an inch. "Or I'll make the driver stop the car."

"Then what?"

"I'll get out."

"And then what?"

She wrinkled her brow, pressing her lips together. She shook her head, and he noticed that half of her hair had come down. He ran his gaze over her, noting a tear at the hem of her dress and that she was missing a shoe and an earring. Things he could replace. If only he could replace her memories and experiences as easily.

Her expression opened up, slowly returning to the Lucy he'd known before. "No, I'll kick *you* out of the car."

"What if I refuse to get out?"

"You won't."

"Why?"

"You just wouldn't."

He sat back in his seat, the boiling-hot mess of emotions slowly draining from him. Maybe she did know the difference between him and that asshole. Somewhere deep inside she knew the difference. At least he hoped to hell she did.

"You're right on that, darlin'. I'd get out if you told me to. I'd do just about anything you told me to do." Did she know? Did she have any idea the power she held over him? He reckoned if she did, she'd never truly believe it.

"I'm sorry," she said.

"I swear to Jesus if you say that one more time, I *will* get out of this fucking car. I'm the one who should be apologizing. I'm sorry."

"Do you realize that since we got married you curse more?"

Did he? He supposed it was because there was so fucking much to curse about. "Does it bother you? I'll stop."

"Maybe if you saved it for the bedroom."

He let out a half laugh. "You want me to talk dirty to you, darlin'? You'd like that?"

She nodded, a naughty gleam in her eyes. "Isn't that one of the options?"

"If not, we'll add it."

She smiled, and it was like the first rays of sunlight across the open water, lighting up everything inside him. She sat up, and her fear seemed to fall away. "I do know you're not like...him. I know it in my heart—" She placed a hand on her chest. "But it's going to take time for my head to catch up. I'm—" She made a noise at the back of her throat. "I *regret* that you're the one paying the price for what he did to me."

"Darlin', that's the same as saying you're sorry, and I told you to stop apologizing to me for that asshole. He'll get what he's got coming to him. Don't you worry about that."

"You think so?"

"I know so. Now come here." He held a hand out to her. "I want to hold my wife."

She came right to him, which was something of a relief. He realized that a part of him still expected her to reject him. Maybe he wasn't the only one who needed to relearn how to react. His confidence where she was concerned had taken a hit of his own making. As she curled up in his lap, laying her head on his chest, he swore he'd do everything in his power to protect her and what they were building between them. She'd gifted him with so many things—their daughter, their new life together, and tentative forward moments like this in which he could imagine them together forever.

As the limo pulled through the gates of their home, he swore he'd kill the bastard who was trying to take all of that away.

7

Lucy prepared for the interview with *Dallas Women Today* magazine the way she used to gear up before cheerleading her high school's football games—extra deodorant, Vaseline on her teeth, and double-stick tape on her blouse so she didn't show anything she didn't want shown. Cal had been called out of town unexpectedly to handle problems with a merger or something or other. He'd promised he'd be home in time for the interview, but as it grew closer to the time when the crew was supposed to arrive, the chance that he'd make it grew less and less probable.

Since the night of the ball there had been a subtle shift in their relationship. If she'd asked Cal about it, he'd only deny it. But she felt it. Something had changed between them that she couldn't quite pin down what it was. Nothing was missing that had been there before and nothing had been added. It was more of a rearrangement of things, a slight resorting and reorganizing.

If she had to put a finger on any one thing that had changed, it would be the way Cal seemed to hesitate for a fraction of a second before he spoke to her or reached for her. Almost as though he had to think twice about what he did with her. And then he'd say or do what he'd normally say or do and she'd wonder if it had been her imagination. He was still the same Cal just with a half-second delay.

Earlier that day she'd gotten the best news she'd received in a long time. She was officially HIV free, as was Poppy. She hoped that bit of good news might shake loose the doubts that seemed to lurk at the back of her brain. She and Cal didn't have to use condoms anymore if they didn't want to. And they could do other things. Cal had said more than once how he couldn't wait to go down on her. One night he'd described so vividly what he would do to her with his mouth that she practically came right then and there. And she could reciprocate. They could finally cross off option number four.

"Mrs. Sellers?"

Lucy had been so fixated on her sexual daydream that she hadn't heard their housekeeper, Hazel, come into the room. She had a feeling that wasn't the first time Hazel had called to her from the doorway of Lucy's bedroom.

"I'm sorry, Hazel. What is it?"

"Priscilla Barnes from *Dallas Women Today* is here with a photographer for your interview. Miss Preston has them setting up in the living room."

"Thank you. I'll be right down."

Lucy gave herself one last look in the mirror, then squared her shoulders and followed Hazel down the stairs. Cal's publicist, Charity Preston, had arrived early that morning with a small crew of hair and makeup people. Everything Lucy was wearing had been chosen by Charity and deemed appropriate for Cal Sellers's new wife. Lucy must give the right impression. Appearance was everything to Charity. Even if it was fake, which described perfectly how Charity's hair and makeup people had made Lucy look.

Before entering the living room, Lucy took a deep breath and let it out slowly. Then she swept into the room as Charity had shown her how to do and walked straight up to Priscilla Barnes, offering her hand.

"Ms. Barnes, it's a pleasure to meet you."

The woman gave her a funny look.

"*I'm* Priscilla Barnes."

Lucy swung around to find Charity glaring at her as she stood next to a woman who was clearly Priscilla Barnes...twenty-five years older and without all of the retouching of the photo Charity had shown her of the woman. Oh, crud. There was no making up for this. Charity had drilled into Lucy how important it was that she greet Priscilla just so and give her as much attention as possible. Lucy had failed on both accounts. Miserably.

"Of course," Lucy stammered as she made her way over. "I'd know you anywhere. Please forgive my mistake." She held her hand out to Priscilla, catching Charity shaking her head out of the corner of her eye. Crap. She'd messed up again. Priscilla was a germaphobe. She hated shaking hands. Lucy quickly disguised the gesture as an all-encompassing sweep of her hand around the room. "Welcome to my home, Ms. Barnes."

Priscilla ran her gaze over Lucy, then the room in general. After what felt like forever, her pale blue stare returned to Lucy, pinning her to the carpet with its directness. "You have a lovely home, Mrs. Sellers. You must be very proud of yourself."

Of all the insulting things! Not that Lucy should be

proud of her home, but of the way in which she'd acquired it, insinuating that she'd attained it by lying on her back. Lucy wanted to tell the insufferable cow that she *was* proud, proud of the way she was able to hold back and not coldcock the bitch.

Charity must have seen something in Lucy's face because she stepped in smoothly with, "Mrs. Sellers, why don't you have a seat on the sofa." She beckoned the makeup artist. "Wanda, can you give Mrs. Sellers a little touch-up?"

Charity steered Priscilla away from Lucy by asking the woman a question about where Priscilla had just returned from vacation. A question Lucy had been coached to ask. Lucy hadn't been in the room half a minute before she'd botched the whole thing. She dropped onto the sofa and lifted her chin so Wanda could sweep a makeup brush across her face.

Lucy had one job. One. To make Cal look good. She couldn't seem to do that one simple thing. He'd asked her to do this interview in the hope it would present Lucy to the Dallas business community as his wife and earn her some much-needed good press. And she'd gone and mucked it up big time. How was she going to make this up to him?

The front door opened and closed, and Cal came striding into the living room. He spotted Lucy and paused for that half second before heading toward her. Lucy caught Priscilla's raised eyebrow and Charity's pressed lips as she stood to greet her husband. So they'd noticed Cal's hesitation too. Great. Just great.

"Sorry I'm late, darlin'." Cal bent and kissed Lucy on the cheek. He put his mouth to her ear and whispered, "You'll be fine."

Cal gave her elbow a squeeze and turned to make his way toward Priscilla and Charity. "Damned if you don't get prettier and prettier every time I see you, Priscilla. I hope you're not giving Charity too much grief over the setup here."

"No, Cal, it's fine. I understand perfectly why your new bride would want to show off her new home." Priscilla sent Lucy a smile that dripped with the condescension she'd laced through her words.

"Now don't go blaming Lucy." Cal returned to his wife and brought her over into their group. "This was all my idea." He looked down at her with all the love she felt from him in their most private moments, and it made her cheeks heat. "I want the world to see what I see when I look at her. She's the best wife and mother a husband could ask for. And that's never more apparent than when we're in our home."

The real reason was because they could control the environment and who had access to Lucy. But if Priscilla Barnes knew that, she'd know how real the rumors were about Lucy. The last thing they needed was more fodder for the rumor mill.

Lucy pasted on her best *Pleasure at Home* smile and hugged her husband around the waist. "And you're the best father and husband a wife could ask for."

"Darlin', that's hardly true, but I love you for saying it." He kissed Lucy's forehead.

"Well." Priscilla clapped her hands together. "Shall we get started then? Or do the two of you need a...moment?"

"What I have in mind for my wife will certainly take longer than a moment." Cal winked at Priscilla, which seemed to have little effect on the woman.

They were doomed. This whole scheme to redeem

Lucy in the public's opinion was going to backfire on them. She should call this whole thing off right now and save herself the humiliation of what Priscilla would write about her. And about Cal.

Charity cleared her throat. "Mr. and Mrs. Sellers, why don't you have a seat on the couch." Charity motioned toward the chair next to the sofa. "Ms. Barnes. Can I get anyone anything before we get started? A beverage maybe?"

"Nothing for me," Priscilla said before lowering herself gingerly onto the chair. She placed her hands in her lap over her tablet and narrowed herself, as though she was trying to touch as little of the chair as possible.

"Lucy?" Cal asked.

Lucy shook her head and arranged her skirt so that it lay smoothly in her lap. "Nothing for me, thank you."

"We're fine, Charity." Cal unbuttoned his suit jacket and stretched back, placing an arm around Lucy.

"I can see you're still in the honeymoon phase of your marriage," Priscilla began, tapping her tablet to life. "How did the two of you meet?"

For all of her ferociousness and judgmental behavior, Priscilla Barnes conducted the interview like a professional. It was almost as if all the questions had been given to her in advance and were slanted strongly toward making Lucy look good. Priscilla lobbed so many slow-pitched questions Lucy's way that Lucy forgot why she was supposed to keep her guard up. After a rough start, Priscilla seemed to really warm toward Lucy.

Maybe warm was too generous a word. Priscilla had stopped looking down her nose at Lucy as if she were the source of whatever horrid mysterious scent Priscilla thought she smelled. Even Charity had relaxed back in her chair. Lucy began to think that maybe she hadn't messed things up for Cal after all, that maybe this interview would be the boon they needed for Cal's reputation.

Priscilla powered off her tablet. "That's all I have. Thank you for being such interesting interview subjects. Marcus." She motioned for the photographer. "Why don't you get some posed shots of Mr. and Mrs. Sellers? Then maybe we can convince them to bring in their daughter for some family photos."

Wanda moved in with her makeup brushes. When she was finished, the photographer directed them how to sit and where to look and began snapping away.

After a few moments, Priscilla called a halt. "And now the little girl."

Lucy started to stand, but Cal motioned her back down. "I'll get her."

Charity got a phone call that she left the room to take, leaving Lucy alone with Priscilla.

As soon as Charity was out of the room, Priscilla pounced like a hundred-and-twenty-pound cat dressed in Chanel. "As I understand it, you got married as a business arrangement, a deal just like all the others he negotiates on a daily basis."

Lucy couldn't hold back her surprise. How did Priscilla know that their marriage had started as a business deal? Lucy looked around the room for some help, but the only other people in the room were the photographer and Priscilla's assistant huddled together discussing the next shots.

"I..." Lucy began.

"I also understand that he's asked for a paternity test on the child."

Lucy jerked back as though the woman had slapped her. Cal wanted a paternity test?

"And that there was no prenup. Rather clever of you, *Mrs. Sellers*." Priscilla said the words *Mrs. Sellers* in a tone that branded Lucy a whore. "Although if the child turns out to not be his, you might have some trouble on your hands." Priscilla leaned forward and delivered a shot that went straight through Lucy. "All of your bedroom tricks might not be enough to hold on to him, but I'm sure you'll be able to console yourself with half his fortune."

Lucy gasped so loud the other two people in the room turned her way. Cal reentered the room with a big smile on his face, carrying Poppy. "She said my name."

"How wonderful," Priscilla said as she rose to her feet. "She's just darling. But isn't she a little young yet to be talking?"

Lucy sat, unable to move, pinned to the couch by Priscilla's words. If Priscilla knew about them, then it was all going to come crashing down around them. Cal would never redeem his reputation if Priscilla wrote about their arrangement in the magazine. It would be all over Dallas about how his marriage wasn't real, that it was a business deal. Or worse, that he'd paid Lucy to be his wife. He'd become the butt of cruel jokes. He was better off with a reputation as a playboy than as a man who paid women to be with him.

"I distinctly heard her say 'da'," Cal said.

"Babies make all kinds of gibberish sounds." Priscilla leaned in for a closer look at Poppy, no doubt checking to see if there was any resemblance between Cal and his daughter. "What lovely red hair she has." But Priscilla didn't sound like she thought it was lovely. More like a smoking gun that confirmed her suspicions about Lucy.

"She gets that from her momma's— Darlin', are you all right?" Cal brushed past Priscilla to get to Lucy, making the woman jump out of the way to avoid any contact with Poppy.

Lucy cleared her throat and put on a smile that hurt almost as much as the knot twisting her gut. "I'm fine. Just a little warm." She stood up. "I'll be right back." She dodged Cal and didn't look at Priscilla as she passed the bitch. She had to get a hold of herself before she broke down in front of Priscilla and really gave that viper a story to publish.

She tried to close the door to the downstairs bathroom, but Cal caught it and stopped her. "Are you feeling all right, darlin'? You're as pale as porcelain."

"I'm fine." She jerked on the handle of the door, fine pricks of sweat popping out all over her body as her mouth filled with saliva. "I'll just be a minute."

Cal dropped his hand, but the look on his face told her that he didn't believe her for a second. Lucy got the door closed and locked seconds before she heaved into the toilet. She reached over and turned on the tap to help disguise the noise. When she got herself under control, she flushed the toilet and rinsed her mouth out.

One look in the mirror and she knew there was no way Cal was going to let this go. He'd know for sure something was wrong. Her skin had gone white beneath the heavy makeup, and her hair had slipped out of some of its pins. She did her best to fix it, but without a brush and some hairspray her efforts did little to hide the fact that she wasn't well.

What was she going to do? There wasn't any kind of spin Charity could put on this that would make it palatable. Lucy could imagine the title of the magazine article

—Local Businessman Buys a Wife. Once the story broke, it would be all over for them. Cal would be humiliated. Ruined. A laughingstock.

Did Cal really not believe that Poppy was his? He could pay for a thousand paternity tests, and they'd all come out the same. Poppy was as much Cal's as she was Lucy's. Why hadn't he told her about his doubts? Had he already had the test done? Or was he only thinking about having it done? The one thing that hadn't changed in the last week or so was Cal's feelings toward Poppy. He'd been just as affectionate, just as smitten as ever, if not more so. Was he planning on telling her about the test? Or was he planning on having it done secretly and only mention it if the results came back that he wasn't the father?

Cal took matters into his own hands and unlocked the door with the spare key. He slipped into the bathroom and found Lucy sitting on the toilet lid, her head in her hands.

He dropped to his knees in front of her, pried her fingers away, and tilted her chin up so he could get a good look at her. "Darlin', what's wrong? What happened?" She blinked up at him, her big blue eyes filled with tears, and it felt like someone had skewered him right through the chest with a hot poker. "Darlin'..." he breathed, hardly able to get the words out. "What is it?"

"She knows."

"Who knows?"

"Priscilla Barnes." A tear slipped through her lower lashes and slid down her cheek, and that hot poker twisted inside him. "She knows about our marriage. Our bargain. Do you really want to get a paternity test? Because you can get one. You can get a thousand of them if you want to. Poppy's yours." More tears streaked down her face. He swiped at them as fast as they fell. "I swear to God she's yours, Cal."

How in the hell had Priscilla Barnes found out about their bargain? He hadn't told anyone, and he knew Lucy hadn't either.

"Oh, darlin'. Is that all?" He tried to make light of it, but he knew as much as Lucy likely did that he was going to take a hard knock when that article hit the newsstands. He could kiss that deal with Gleason and Hadley Investments goodbye. All of his plans, his careful work...gone.

He held her face and put his forehead to hers. "I know she's mine. I don't need any test to tell me that. And even if she weren't, I wouldn't care. I'm so in love with that little girl you'd have a hell of a time separating me from her."

"But what about that deal you've been working on? Marrying me was supposed to improve your reputation, not make it worse. All I've done since we got back together is make things worse for you. I can't even have sex right," she sobbed.

"Darlin', we have the rightest sex that's ever been attempted, let alone accomplished."

"You know what I mean. I can't do the things you want. I can't be the way I was before. I'm broken, and now I'm breaking you."

"The only way you could break me was if you left me."

"We never should've gotten married."

He sat back on his heels, the fury he carried around every day rising up inside him. He would destroy Priscilla Barnes for making Lucy feel this way, for making her cry. "Stay here. Don't move. I'll be right back."

He left the bathroom and went down the hall to his office. Punching in the number for Phil Davies, the publisher of *Dallas Women Today* magazine, Cal tipped some whiskey into a tumbler and managed to get two swallows down before Phil picked up.

"Phil, Cal Sellers here." He charged ahead without waiting for the man to respond to his greeting. "Priscilla Barnes is in my living room. She seems to be operating under the misconception that she's writing for a grocery-store tabloid."

"Sir?"

"Now I can handle the first part of my problem myself. I'm counting on you to handle the second."

"Yes, sir."

"I knew you were the right man for the job. Give your wife my best. Good night."

"Good night, sir."

Cal punched the End button on his cell phone and drained his glass. He didn't throw his weight around often, preferring to let his employees handle their jobs, but every now and then it paid to remind his employees who signed their paychecks. Sellers Investments' ownership of *Dallas Women Today* magazine wasn't well known. He doubted Priscilla Barnes had any idea she'd walked into her employer's house and insulted his wife in the most egregious way possible.

He set the tumbler on his desk and strode back out into the living room, where Priscilla stood a fair distance from her assistant. It took them a moment to realize he'd entered the room.

"I hope your wife is feeling all right," she all but sneered. "Those sudden bouts of *illness* can be difficult."

Cal took her by the elbow. "We've kept you too long. I'm sure you have a lot to do, so don't let us take up any more of your time." Behind him he could hear the photographer and the assistant quickly grabbing their things.

"But—" Priscilla began.

"Thank you again for coming," Charity added, going along with what Cal wanted. She'd worked for him too long not to know when he'd had enough. "We look forward to reading your article." She handed Priscilla her coat and opened the front door.

Priscilla appeared to be so startled by Cal rushing her out the door that she didn't get another word out until she was standing in the driveway and Cal was closing the door on her and her crew. "Thank you, Mr. Sellers. And thank your wife—"

Cal slammed the door on the woman, then rounded on Charity. "I told you that Lucy was not to be alone with that bitch."

"She wasn't. I was in the room the whole... Oh shit. I had to take a call. I was only gone a couple minutes."

"Oh shit, is right." Cal reopened the door and gestured for her to leave. "You're fired."

"But Mr. Sellers...Cal..."

"Goodbye, Charity."

On the porch, Charity turned around. "I'm sorry. I never thought..."

"And that's why you're fired." He slammed the door hard enough to rattle the vase on the entryway table. Then he went in search of his wife.

8

C al found Lucy in the last place he expected to find her—their bedroom closet. She was throwing clothes into a suitcase. The fury that had been simmering ever since he figured out what Priscilla had done to Lucy would've boiled over if not for the biting panic that kicked him in the chest.

"You're not leaving me." He hadn't meant to blurt that out, but there it was—his worst fear.

"I think it's best for everyone involved."

She was so calm, and it was that calmness that scared him more than anything. He could handle the potent emotional brew that seemed to pour from her whether she was happy, sad, or mad. But this serene acceptance ate at his control. He caught a skirt she tried to toss into the suitcase in midair and threw it to the floor.

"I said..." he stalked toward her, backing her up against the clothes hanging in the closet, "...you're not fucking leaving me."

"Cal..."

A part of him registered her fear, but the other part of

him—the part where anger had taken up residence and festered—overrode any instinct he might have had to pull back and rein in his emotions. "We have a deal. One year."

She put a hand on his chest, twisting so her body was partially turned away. It was a defensive move meant to expose as little of her as possible, like a boxer would.

"You promised me one year, Lucy, and you're going to give it to me."

He was crowding her now. She leaned back into the clothes hanging behind her. He shoved the hangers aside, exposing more of her. She wasn't going to hide from him, from this.

When he saw the look on her face, all the fight went out of him. He wasn't that man. He wasn't a bully. He damn sure wasn't like her ex. "I'm sorry." He gave her some room, backing away. "Please. Don't leave me."

She looked up at him from over her shoulder. "I was supposed to help your business reputation." She tilted back a little more, her tone not as calm as before, but at least she didn't sound frightened. "Not hurt it. *That* was the deal."

"Yeah, that was the deal. But do you know what else was part of the deal?"

"What?"

"Keeping you and Poppy safe."

She shifted her feet, turning so she faced him fully once more. "No, it wasn't. I never asked for that."

"It was in our vows."

"Those weren't real. They were just part of what we had to do to seal the deal."

"Maybe they weren't real for you, darlin', but they were damn real for me."

"I don't know why you'd want me around for another

week, let alone the rest of the year. I've ruined everything. Priscilla Barnes is probably right now typing up that article, and it's going to ruin you." She made air quotes. "The Great Cal Sellers Buys a Wife."

He shook his head. He'd been so caught up in Lucy's upset he hadn't paid enough attention to what had happened downstairs. He held up a hand. "Wait a minute. What exactly did that bitch say about our deal?"

"What do you mean?

"Come out of there. I can't have this conversation with you half buried in dresses."

He helped her climb out of the clothes racks and sat next to her on the little sofa thing in the middle of the closet. How much did Priscilla Barnes know about their deal? Did she know that he'd been paying Lucy the whole time they'd been married? Had she somehow tricked Lucy into admitting it?

"What did she say?" he asked. "Exactly. I want to know the exact words she used."

"Well..." She tilted her head to the side. "She kept using the words 'I understand'—I understand this and I understand that. She called our marriage a business arrangement, a deal just like all the others you negotiate. And then she congratulated me on marrying you without a prenup. But you have to know I would never take your money or this house."

"I do know that, darlin'. Although if you did ever leave me, you may as well take everything I have with you because without you I'd have nothing."

"Jesus, Cal. How can you say stuff like that to me after everything I've put you through?"

"Because it's true."

She put a hand on his cheek, bringing his face closer to hers. "I don't want to leave you. But I also don't want to keep making things worse for you." She dropped her hand in her lap on a sigh. "I don't know what to do. I can't stay and I can't leave and I can't fix what I messed up for you."

"Priscilla Barnes's threats have nothing to do with you. You didn't cause what happened today, but I think I know who might have. What did she say about Poppy?"

"Just that she *understood* that you wanted a paternity test. And then she insinuated that all of my bedroom tricks wouldn't be enough to hold on to all of the things I gained by marrying you, like your house and your money, if Poppy wasn't yours."

"She hasn't experienced your bedroom tricks."

She smacked him on the arm. "Be serious."

"I am serious. There's this one thing that you do—"

"I think you should get a paternity test."

"Why in the hell would I do that?"

"Because it would put all of the rumors to rest once and for all about Poppy."

"I haven't gotten to where I am in business and in life by chasing down and quashing random rumors. And I'm not going to start now. No. No paternity test."

"Fine. Then I'll get one."

"You can't get one without a DNA sample from me."

She tossed her hair over her shoulder and gave him that look that sent a shot of lust straight to his groin. "Oh, I can get a DNA sample from you, cowboy."

"Well, damn, darlin', is that a threat or a promise?"

"It's a fact." She climbed onto his lap and wrapped her arms around his neck, her skirt sliding dangerously high up her thighs. He followed it with his hands. "I bet I could get more than one from you in the next hour if I really wanted to," she bragged.

"Prove it."

"Right here in the closet?"

"The closet, the floor, the bed. I don't care where."

She kissed him, and that last sliver of fear dissolved as he slid his hands all the way up her skirt to grab her ass and pull her closer. He didn't know what he'd do if she'd gone through with it and left him. He didn't care what that dried-up bitch thought of him or of Lucy, but he sure as hell cared that it bothered Lucy. She'd been through so goddamned much. The last thing she needed was to worry about what anyone outside this closet thought of them.

He worked a hand up her blouse and popped the hooks on her bra. The feel of her. The fullness that more than filled his hand. Those little sounds of pleasure she made when he did something she liked. He could spend all day every day lying naked with her and exploring her body. All of those uncharted spots. All of those abundant curves.

He'd been so caught up in her that he hadn't noticed her hands had been busy too. She'd unbuttoned his shirt, and she now had her hand on his zipper...then on him. She stroked him slowly...so slowly. Groaning, he pushed up into her hand.

"Option number four," she whispered next to his ear, then she went to her knees in front of him. She bent and licked his cock, sending a shudder through him.

"Yes. Okay. Sure. Whatever you want."

Her smile... Jesus. She leaned forward and took him into her mouth. Deep. He dropped his head back and tried not to think about her full lips sliding up then down the length of him. It had been so long since she'd sucked him off— What the hell?

"What are you *doing*?" He moved back, causing his dick to slip out of her mouth. Her mouth...damn.

She ran her tongue along her lower then upper lip, like a cat licking cream. "It's called giving head."

"I know what it's called. I thought you couldn't do it."

"I couldn't until I knew I was cleared. Poppy's and my final tests came in. Both negative. Now do you want to talk or—?"

Lucy found herself squeezed in the fiercest hug she'd ever had.

"Are you both really okay?" he asked, his voice muffled in the side of her neck.

"Yes. We're both fine. This wasn't exactly the way I wanted to tell you..."

He lifted his head and looked at her. "I don't care. I'm just so damn glad you're both all right."

"We're fine."

"Really?"

"Really."

"In that case..."

In one swift move Cal changed their positions so that she was the one lying on the couch with him on top. He pushed her skirt up, grabbed a hold of her panties, and pulled them off, throwing them over his shoulder.

"If I recall, darlin', option number four is a mutually beneficial option. I get to finally put my mouth here." He slid a finger down her slickness. "Already wet."

"And I get to put *my* mouth here." She reached for him, enjoying the *ugh* her touch elicited. "This couch may not be the best place for this."

"Wrong." He bent and licked her. "You're right where I want you."

He set his mouth to her, slipping one then two fingers into her, stroking deep. She arched back, giving in to him. How could she do anything else? Within a matter of minutes she was so close to coming she thought she'd die if she didn't. Her breath hitched as he slowed then stopped altogether.

"What are you *doing*?"

"Punishing you."

"Punish... What for?"

"For threatening to leave me."

"God, Cal, can we talk—?"

He rubbed her clit with his thumb in practiced strokes.

"Ohh, yesss," she moaned.

He slipped his fingers inside of her again, curling his middle finger so it hit just the right spot... "Promise me."

"Yes."

"You won't leave. Don't even threaten to leave me. Say it." He caught her nipple between his fingers. "Say it and I'll make you come so hard you'll think you've died."

"No, Cal," she panted. She was close. *So* close. "I won't leave... I won't leave you."

He licked her clit, then sucked, increasing the pace of his hands. Her orgasm barreled toward her. She was all sensation. The prickling heat...that tense fingernail edge... the ecstasy of that half-second right before...and then it hit. She screamed, her body bowing under the onslaught. He cupped her, holding the sensations in and drawing them out. She distantly felt her body. It was below her somewhere, heavy and spent. Cal was saying something to her, kissing her neck, her breasts. And then he pressed into her little by little until he hit deep.

The pleasure built again, slower than before. She didn't think she could sustain another orgasm. But the feel of him inside her, on top of her, around her, it was all too much. He mumbled something...endearments and naughty words. The dirtier he talked, the quicker she came back around until she was on the edge of orgasm, urging him on with her cries and her fingers gripping his bare ass. She came on a long, low moan, and he quickly followed, driving deep into her.

"Jesus, God, darlin'."

She let out a heavy sigh. "Yeah."

"Are we dead? Did we kill each other?"

"If this is death, then it beats life by miles."

His chuckle vibrated through her. He traced a finger around her nipple, making the skin around it pucker. "Well, I did promise to make you come so hard you'd think you'd died."

"And you nearly killed us both."

He rose up on his elbow to look down at her. "You're going to keep your promise to me."

"Or what? Every time I try to leave you'll get me naked and make me come so hard I can't walk let alone walk out the door?"

"No." He dropped his gaze to where his hand lay on her breast. "This started out as a business deal, but that's not what it is anymore, is it?"

"Definitely not. Unless you make love to everyone you do business with."

"Hell, no. Although if I did, more deals might go my way."

"*All* the deals would go your way." She fisted a hand in

his hair and brought his head down for a slow-winding kiss that she hoped told him more than she could ever say with words. About how much he meant to her. How much she loved him, wanted him, *craved* him. And how grateful she was to have him in hers and Poppy's lives.

When they parted, he gave her a look that she'd never seen on him before, and then it was gone and in its place was his usual wicked grin. "Keep kissing me like that and you're going to get your second DNA sample."

"I wasn't kidding when I told you I think you should get that paternity test."

"Darlin', don't talk about paternity tests while I'm still inside you. You'll jinx us." He shifted to lie next to her.

"You don't want another baby?"

"Sure I do. I thought maybe you'd want to wait till Poppy's a little older."

She shrugged. "I'm on birth control, but if it happens, it happens. I actually would like to wait. Maybe until next year."

"Until we're past our one-year mark?"

"Something like that."

He lifted her chin with his finger so she had to look up at him. "Something like what? Be honest."

"I guess I just want to make sure we're as strong as we can be before we bring another child into the world. And that it's a safe world."

He studied her for a moment, his wild blue eyes searching for something. Maybe that tiny seed of doubt she still carried where he was concerned. He'd changed a lot since they'd been together before. In big and in small ways. The memory of him bending his secretary over his desk still haunted her sometimes, only now the memories were of people she hardly recognized anymore. They weren't the same people they'd been the first time around.

They wouldn't make the same mistakes.

"I want to make sure Kevin can't hurt us ever again," she said. "I can't bring another child into this nightmare."

"I agree." He looked like he was going to say something more, but then nuzzled her neck instead. "About that second DNA sample…"

9

"Lucy, let's go," Cal hollered up the stairs. "We're going to be late if we don't leave in the next five minutes."

"I'm coming!"

Ten minutes later Lucy came barreling down the stairs, her shoes and purse in one hand and two presents in the other. Cal met her halfway and relieved her of her packages.

"Two presents?"

She slipped her shoes on. "One for Crosby and one for Mi."

Cal eyed the packages as he held the front door open for his wife. He knew Rob Crosby, the director of *Pleasure at Home*, had specifically requested no gifts. "What did you get for Crosby?"

"Scotch."

"Good call."

He helped her into the car, and then they were finally on their way to the party. He'd lied when he'd told her they had five minutes, padding their timing by fifteen minutes. And it was a good thing he did. He hated being late, even to a retirement party/baby shower.

"I can't believe Crosby's retiring. I thought for sure he'd keel over in his director's chair at ninety-three while yelling at one of the grips."

Cal had promised Crosby he wouldn't tell anyone the real reason Crosby was retiring early—he had terminal cancer and wanted to spend his last days with his family. It hadn't been an easy thing, making that promise to his friend or keeping it. Lucy had worked with Crosby for two years. If she knew he was keeping this info about Crosby from her, she'd be very upset with him. And the last thing he wanted was his wife upset with him.

Things between them for the past few weeks had been really good. Incredible. The article about Lucy had been published with a completely different slant than he imagined Priscilla Barnes had had in mind. But then, her name hadn't appeared in the byline.

They hadn't heard a thing from Lucy's asshole ex, and Cal had begun to wonder if maybe he wasn't gearing up for something. Of course he didn't share his concerns with Lucy. She had started to hope that maybe Walker had lost interest. Lucas had been keeping an eye out, and so far Walker hadn't shown up on any police blotter or in any morgue. He was still out there...somewhere.

They drove up to the TV station where *Pleasure at Home* was filmed, which looked like every other office building in the industrial park it was located in. Lucy jumped out of the car before Cal threw it into park, excited to be seeing her old friends again. He angled out of the car and slid on his Stetson, pulling it low to shade his eyes. He got the presents out of the backseat and jogged to catch up to his wife.

"I'm thinking we need to get you out of the house more often, darlin', if you're this starved for company that you'd leave me behind to carry your packages."

Lucy slipped her arm through Cal's. "It feels like forever since I've seen Mi, and it has absolutely been forever since I've seen Crosby and the rest of the crew. I have good memories here, Cal. Working here was one of the highlights of my life...other than having Poppy."

"And marrying me."

"Well, yes. And that too. Of course."

He laughed. She always made him laugh. And kept him honest.

They entered the studio to find the party in full swing. Lucy broke away to greet her friends. Cal spotted Lucas off to the side leaning against the wall. After handing the presents off to one of the production assistants, he headed for his friend.

Cal had met Lucas so many years ago, he'd lost track of how long they'd known each other. Lucas was Cal's opposite in just about every way, but somehow their friendship worked. Cal had learned long ago not to question the why of it. He was so damn lucky to have a friend like Lucas.

"Hey," he said.

"Hey," Lucas replied.

"Where'd you get that beer?"

Lucas reached into the cooler next to him, pulled out a beer, and handed it to Cal.

"Thanks. Looks like the wives are glad to see each other."

Across the room Lucy and Mi were embracing and crying like they hadn't seen each other in years.

"Mi's been so busy training Elisa and getting ready for the baby she hasn't had much spare time."

"I hear your sister's a natural at selling sex toys," Cal teased.

Lucas made a face. "I owe you a punch in the throat for hiring her."

"She's a grown woman. Attractive. Smart. The audience loves her. You should be happy. With Elisa taking over the show, Mi will have more time to spend with you and the baby when he comes."

"You're not the only one to notice my sister's attractiveness," Lucas grumbled.

Cal tracked his friend's gaze across the room to where *Pleasure at Home*'s new director, Ian Kershaw, stood talking to one of the cameramen. Only Kershaw's gaze wasn't on the man in front of him—it was firmly latched on to Elisa's ass. Cal could hardly blame the man. Lucas's sister had caught Cal's eye a time or two back in the day. Tall like the rest of the Vegas, Elisa had long dark hair, exotic looks, a nice firm ass, and a rack any man would love to get his hands on. And it looked like that was exactly what Ian Kershaw had in mind.

Cal chuckled. "Like I said...she's a grown woman."

"Don't you have some kind of rule about romance in the workplace you could enforce?"

"It'd be hypocritical of me, seeing as how I slept with Lucy when she was the host of *Pleasure at Home*." Cal tipped his beer toward Lucas. "And of you too, since I do believe you were in my employ when you took up with Mi. Moved her right into your house *and* your bed."

Lucas shifted his feet. "That doesn't count. Damn. He's coming our way."

Ian Kershaw made his way across the room to where Lucas and Cal stood. Elisa followed his movement, *her* gaze firmly on *Kershaw's* ass.

"Looks like the attraction's mutual." Cal clapped his friend on the shoulder and laughed. "Be nice. Kershaw could end up being your brother-in-law."

"Fuck off," Lucas muttered.

"Hello, Mr. Sellers." Ian held his hand out, and Cal shook it. "Thanks again for the opportunity here at *Pleasure at Home*."

"Call me Cal." He gestured toward Lucas. "Have you met Lucas Vega, Mi's husband...and Elisa's brother?"

"No, I don't believe we've met." Ian shook Lucas's hand, managing to not grimace at the excessive force Lucas used. "Nice to meet you."

Lucas grunted.

Despite Lucas's feelings toward the man, Cal was grateful to have him aboard. Just when Cal thought they'd never find a new director for the show, Ian Kershaw's resume had come across his desk. Ian was overqualified for the job, and in accepting it took a pay cut. Cal had Lucas check out Kershaw, and he couldn't find any reason why the man would take a career step down to move from California to Dallas. He'd left his last job in L.A. with a glowing recommendation from a popular reality TV show's producer, sold his home in Malibu, and moved to Texas where—according to Lucas's report on the man— he had no friends or family.

"You're all settled in then?" Cal asked.

"We start taping the new shows with Elisa as the host next week. I've already been over the marketing plan, and the new products have arrived. Mr. Crosby's been invaluable in helping me get to know everyone and how things work. Everything's set."

"Glad to hear it."

"Hello, gentlemen." Elisa slid in between Cal and Ian. She nodded at her brother. "Lucas."

"Your brother's more of a gentleman than I am," Cal said, smiling despite Lucas's scowl. Cal gave Elisa a hug and a kiss on the cheek. "I guess this is my official chance to welcome you to *Pleasure at Home.*"

Elisa had swept into the studio and delivered an audition that blew everyone away, including Crosby. And he wasn't easy to please. Lucas, on the other hand, had not been pleased. It was one thing for his wife to sell sex toys on TV, and quite another for his sister to do it.

After watching Elisa's tapes, there was no way Cal was going to bend to his friend's wishes. Elisa was a natural. She glowed on camera the same way Mi and Lucy had, only Elisa had a little something more. Cal couldn't put his finger on what exactly that something was, but he heard the sound of cash being sorted while he watched Elisa, and he was sold.

"Thank you. I absolutely love it here. It's my dream job."

Lucas curled his lip at his sister. "Your dream job is touching fake cocks all day?"

"It was good enough for your wife." She gestured toward Cal. "And his wife. But it's not good enough for me? I'm not a virgin, you know, Lucas. I've had sex. I *have* sex. I've even tried out some of those fake cocks. They're pretty darn good. If they could earn a paycheck and rub my feet, I wouldn't need a man at all."

Lucas glanced up at the ceiling, exasperation with his

sister in his body language and tone. "Jesus fucking Christ."

Cal noticed Ian sneaking a side glance at Elisa, an amused smirk on his face. Was he who Elisa was currently having sex with? Or working toward having sex with? That would be some fast work. For all of the ribbing he gave Lucas and how attractive Elisa was, Cal had only ever seen her as the sister of his best friend. Hell, she was almost a sister to him. He made a note to keep an eye on the situation. Not that Lucas wouldn't. But Cal had enough distance from Elisa to see things her brother might overlook. And if Elisa knew Cal intended to play honorary brother to her, she'd probably try to kick his ass.

"We can always count on you, Elisa, to tell it like it is." Cal clinked his beer bottle against hers.

Lucas let out a frustrated sigh and turned to walk away. "I'm going to go find Mi."

"He's seen stuff while in the Navy that the rest of us can't begin to imagine, and yet Lucas gets all puritanical when it comes to sex." Elisa watched her brother put his arm around his wife. "If Mi wasn't pregnant, I'd wonder if he ever has sex at all."

"Give him a break," Ian said. "No man wants to imagine his sister having sex."

"Your sister has three kids," Elisa shot back.

"Immaculate conception." Ian took a sip from his cup.

Cal noticed that the man wasn't drinking alcohol, unless the clear liquid in his cup was straight vodka. He doubted it. Cal's daddy had taught him three things—never trust a woman who only talked about money, never trust a horse showing the whites of its eyes, and never trust a man with something to hide. And something told him that Ian Kershaw had something to hide. Something more than his affair or intended affair with Elisa.

"Welcome aboard, both of you. I'm looking forward to the new shows. If you'll excuse me, I'm going to find my wife."

Cal left the couple whispering to each other and trying—but failing miserably—at hiding their attraction. He looked around for Lucy, but she was nowhere in sight. He'd made sure that security was tighter than usual. As *Pleasure at Home* seemed to attract more than its fair share of negative attention—some of it threatening—there was always security on the premises. Especially since Mi had been the target of a stalker, and the original building the studio had been in had been blown up by a religious extremist group.

There was no reason for Cal to panic. Lucy was probably in the ladies' room and would be back shortly. In the meantime, he'd keep an eye on his assistant, Felicia. That business with Priscilla Barnes had revealed a leak in Cal's otherwise-tight ship. And that leak went by the name of Felicia. She'd been acting strange ever since Cal had gotten married. Her flirting, always easy to ignore, had become more brazen. She'd rub up against any part of Cal she could whenever she could. And her clothes bordered on breaking company policy. But she never did anything that would give him cause to let her go.

There had only been two people in his office when he had proposed the marriage deal to Lucy—him and Lucy. Cal hadn't given a thought to the fact that Felicia had been on the other side of the door. He certainly hadn't figured her for bugging his office, but when he had Lucas do a sweep after the magazine interview, they found one. Not only had Lucas found the listening device, but he was able to track it back to Felicia. Cal wasn't sure if she was working for someone else or if she was using the info she acquired for her own gain. Either way, Felicia was a problem that needed to be solved. He hadn't gotten where he was by acting too fast or in anger. So he was biding his time, watching Felicia, trying to figure out what her game was and making plans to move against her.

Felicia caught him looking at her, said something to the woman she'd been talking to, and headed over to where Cal was. She was attractive and—if he was honest—that had been part of the reason he'd hired her. She'd also come highly recommended and was a very experienced executive assistant.

"Hello, boss." Felicia fingered his tie, stroking her thumb along a nonexistent wrinkle. "Nice party."

He ran a hand down his tie, causing her to drop her hand. "Thanks. I'm glad you're having a good time." He looked out over the top of her head for Lucy. "Did you come here with anyone?"

"No." She angled closer, smashing her breast against his side. "I'm available."

He shifted away. "Have you seen my wife?"

"I think she went to the restroom. She looked a little sick."

Cal made a move to go around her, but she stopped him with a hand on his arm. "I'm sure she's fine. Her friend went with her. Probably all of this rich food." She pulled at him so that he turned toward her. "I don't know about you, but I could use a drink."

The phrase *Keep your friends close and your enemies even closer* came to mind. "What are you having?"

"Whatever you are."

LUCY SPLASHED cold water on her face. She hadn't felt this sick this suddenly since...oh, God. She did some quick mental calculations and realized she should've gotten her period yesterday. She'd been so caught up in everything that had been going on she hadn't been paying attention to the little things. Like when her period was due. She was on birth control, so it should've come right on schedule. Even without birth control, her cycle was predictable practically to the minute.

She and Cal had talked briefly about having another baby. She'd gotten the impression Cal wanted to wait. Jinx them was right. Cal had joked about not talking about babies while he was still inside her, and that was probably the exact moment he'd gotten her pregnant. Damn it. She hadn't lost all of the weight from her first pregnancy, and here she was pregnant again.

Maybe she was overreacting.

She grabbed a handful of towels and blotted her face. Maybe she ate something that didn't agree with her. Maybe all of the stress had made her late. Maybe, maybe, maybe.

Placing a hand on her stomach, she closed her eyes. She was pregnant. She just knew it. That was the kind of luck she had. No sooner had she and Cal stopped doubling up on birth control, she got pregnant. Damn that man. Well, she guessed they'd make it work somehow. And if she dared to admit it, she was secretly glad. Poppy would have a brother or sister, and Cal would get to be there when his child came into the world—something he'd missed with Poppy.

Tears filled her eyes. She reached into her purse for a tissue. Behind her she heard someone come in and then the snick of the lock. She spun around to find Kevin standing just feet away from her.

"Hello, Lucy."

10

"How did you get in here?" Lucy's heart pounded so hard she thought her ribs would crack.

Kevin leaned back against the door and ran his filthy gaze over her. He was dressed in the uniform of the catering company with a long-haired wig and a full fake beard. But she'd know him anywhere. He filled the corners of her mind, always lurking, always invading moments of her life where he didn't belong. Sometimes she even thought she saw him or heard him calling for her. She'd imagined a thousand times what she would say or do when she saw him.

Facing him now, she realized those moments hadn't prepared her. Everything she had thought to say or do fled her mind, leaving behind a frozen stillness and abject helplessness. She had no defense against him. He'd found her. She'd known he would. He would never give up until he got what he wanted. And what he wanted was her dead.

"Still fat," he sneered. "Dressed better though. A fancy pig in billionaire's clothing."

He came off the door and stalked toward her. She backed up against the sinks, the edge of the counter biting into her flesh.

"You can dress a pig up, but it's still a pig. Does he lift that fancy dress and pork you, pig?" He snorted at his own joke.

It was his laugh that Lucy had grown to fear most. He could do almost anything when he was amused. Like a bomb with a lit fuse Lucy never knew when he'd blow. It was the waiting that ate at her. He could explode at any minute, but until he did she kept a small hope that this would be the one time when he wouldn't.

"I'm...I'm not a pig."

His face that she'd thought so handsome once now creased into a frown. He wasn't used to her standing up to him. She'd never talked back when they were together.

He leaned closer. "What did you say, pig?"

"Get out, Kevin."

"Oh, you're giving me orders now?" He grabbed a fistful of her hair. Shaking her by it, he asked, "*You're* giving me orders, you rich, fat pig?"

Spittle dotting his chin, his face red, he crowded her, using his size and strength against her. She could see the explosion was near. He twisted her hair in his fist, and she grimaced in pain, biting back a cry.

"Just because you're fucking a billionaire doesn't give you the right to give me orders." He caught her under her chin with his other hand. "I could kill you. I could fuck you and kill you. You're *nothing*."

His fingers pressed into her neck on either side of her windpipe. He'd done this many times before—make her black out then wait for her to come back around so he could do it all over again. Sometimes she'd wake up with him on top of her, raping her. Sometimes she'd wake up locked in the closet or the bedroom. He'd torment her from the other room, making her feel small...*making* her nothing.

Her purse was trapped between their bodies, her hand inside wrapped around a packet of tissues. She shoved her hand in deeper. Dots filled her vision as he lifted her. Blackness feathered the edges of her sight, narrowing in on his face so close to hers.

"Lu-cyyy," he chanted. "Lu-cyyy, Lu-cyyy—"

A muffled bang made them both freeze. Kevin's eyes widened as his grip on her loosened. He released her, putting the hand he'd had on her throat over the blood seeping out of his stomach. He stared at her in shock.

"Lucy?"

She pulled the trigger again. He pitched back, releasing her entirely. She gripped the edge of the counter and fired again. And again. And again until the gun clicked empty. She kept pulling the trigger until her knees gave way and she spiraled downward. The last image she saw was of Kevin lying on the floor, a pool of blood leaking out from under him onto the tile.

Then nothing.

AT THE SOUND OF SHOTS, everyone in the room froze. And then pandemonium. Lucas gave Cal a look that said *stay back* as he pulled a gun from the small of his back. The hell he would. Lucas moved in the direction of where the gunshots had come from. Cal didn't hesitate. He raced after his friend. All he could think was Lucy...Lucy... *Where is Lucy*?

They hit the hall together. Cal cursed himself for not bringing his own gun. A couple of the security guys pounded on a closed door. The women's restroom.

"Lucy!" Cal shouted. "Lucy!"

Lucas rammed the metal door with his shoulder, but it didn't budge. "Somebody get a key!" He began to beat at the lock with the butt of his gun.

Cal spotted a fire extinguisher down the hall. He ran over, pushing partygoers out of the way, and grabbed the extinguisher. He took over smashing the lock until it bent and gave.

Lucas put a hand on Cal's chest, stopping him from rushing in. Gun drawn, Lucas eased the door open, going in low. "Somebody call an ambulance!"

Lucas ran in with Cal right on his heels. Lucy lay on the floor under the sinks, her gun in her hand. Next to her Walker lay still. Lucy must've put every single one of her bullets in him. Lucas went for Walker, and Cal went for Lucy. He dropped to his knees next to her and checked her pulse, nearly collapsing on top of her when he felt it strong and sure. Everything he ever wanted and didn't deserve was right there in front of him. If anything ever happened to her, he didn't know what he'd do.

He stroked her cheek. "Lucy. Lucy. Come on, darlin', wake up for me."

"Oh, my God!" Mi rushed over and knelt next to Cal. "Is she okay? Is she going to be okay?" She reached for Lucy's hand and rubbed it between both of hers. "Lucy. Wake up. Wake up, Lucy."

"He's dead," Lucas announced.

Cal could see the purple impressions of that bastard's hand on Lucy's neck. If he weren't already dead, Cal would've killed Walker himself.

"Darlin'—" His voice cracked. "Open your eyes."

Lucy moaned, and the whole room seemed to let out a collective breath.

"An ambulance is on the way," one of the security guards informed them.

"Oh, thank God," Mi whispered, tears streaking her face. "Thank God."

Lucy moaned again and turned her head toward Cal. Her lips moved, but she didn't make any sound. Her eyelids fluttered open, and Cal stared down into the most beautiful set of blue eyes he'd ever seen.

He swallowed back the emotion that had his chest in a vise grip. "Hey there, darlin'."

"Cal? Where—?" She tried to sit up.

"Stay down until the ambulance gets here," Lucas ordered. "Everyone else out of the room. This is a crime scene. That includes you, *querida*," he said to Mi.

"I'm staying," she told him.

"*Querida...*" Lucas seemed not to know what to do with his wife. "You're pregnant," he pleaded.

"I'm not leaving her." Mi slipped her sweater off and gently tucked it under Lucy's head. When she pulled her hand away, there was blood on it. She balled her hand and quickly hid it from Lucy's view.

Cal thought he might be sick, seeing Lucy's blood on Mi's hand. It could too easily have been Lucy lying in a pool of her own blood, her body riddled with bullets.

"Is he dead?" Lucy asked.

"He's dead all right," Mi answered before Cal could get a word in. "You filled him full of lead. Since when do you know how to shoot a gun?"

Lucy waved a hand toward her husband. "Cal got it for me."

Mi gave him a look that told him she was impressed with him. "I had my doubts about you. I thought you were going to break her heart. Thank you." She threw her arms around him and nearly made him hit his head on one of the sinks. "Thank you for taking care of Lucy and for getting her that gun."

He hugged her back and whispered in her ear, "I'd do anything for her."

When Mi pulled away, she had a whole new look on her face. "I think you'll do," she told him as she patted his cheek.

Police and paramedics came into the room. Lucas finally got Mi to leave Lucy's side and ushered her out with a gentle hand on the small of her back. To see his big, giant friend defer to his much smaller wife made Cal smile.

Lucy didn't want to go to the hospital, but Cal talked her into it. He didn't like the way her head wouldn't stop bleeding and how dizzy she was when they sat her up.

"I'm fine," she complained.

"Humor me. And while we're there, I think I'll have them check me out for signs of a heart attack. I'm pretty sure I had a massive one after seeing you on the floor, darlin'."

"Is he really dead?" Lucy must've asked that about twenty times from when she woke up until they released her from the hospital a few hours later.

The police had taken her statement at the hospital and confiscated her gun, which was fine with Cal as there was no more need for it now that Walker was dead. As soon as they walked in the front door of their home, Lucy demanded to see Poppy when she should've gone in and laid down. Cal had called Sam from the ambulance and had him put Poppy on screen so they could both see for themselves that their daughter was okay. Cal helped her up the stairs and kept her from running up them like she seemed to want to do. He waited for her to sit down before handing her Poppy to hold.

She looked Poppy over from her toes to the top of her head. Cal guessed she was checking to be sure there wasn't a mark on her. She folded Poppy into a fierce hug that made the child squeak before bursting into tears with her face pressed into Poppy's neck. Sam eased out of the room and shut the door behind him.

Cal knelt and embraced his wife and child.

They'd come so close to losing everything. Knowing they were now safe from Walker was overwhelming. He hadn't realized how much tension and anger he'd been holding in, but now it came rushing at him. He held on to his little family, buffeted by one wave of emotion after another.

"He can never hurt you again. He can never hurt any of us ever again. You stopped him, darlin'." He swept her hair back from her face and kissed her wet cheek. "You did it."

"I couldn't have done it without you. Thank you. Thank you for giving me the confidence to believe in something better for myself and for Poppy. And for giving me the strength to stand up to him. I looked him right in the eye, and I stood up for myself. I was never able to strike back before."

"You had it in you all along. If I did anything, it was to help you find the courage you already possessed."

"This isn't like you. The Cal I know isn't modest."

She had a teasing tone to her voice and the first real smile—one with no worry hovering in the background —that he'd seen on her since before he'd messed things up and caused their split. He hadn't noticed the difference until this moment. It was like looking at a picture and not knowing what was different about it until someone pointed it out and then it became painfully obvious.

"I've been brought to my knees and humbled. Everything you've been through can all be laid at my door. And don't think for a moment that I don't know it. Seeing you on the floor of that bathroom, I did drop to my knees. I'm just so grateful for you—" he kissed her, "—and for you." He kissed his daughter's head, which was nestled in the crook of her mother's shoulder.

"Stop." Lucy fanned her face, her eyes filling with tears. "I finally stopped crying, and now you're making me start up all over again."

"No more crying, darlin'. No more fear, no more worry. Nothing but good times ahead."

"And no more extra security. We can take Poppy out of the house. Oh! What about a vacation?"

"I think that's—"

Someone knocked on the door. Cal rose and opened it to find their housekeeper, Hazel, on the other side.

"You have a phone call, Mr. Sellers."

"Who is it?"

"Mr. Gleason. He's calling to confirm dinner tomorrow night."

Cal looked to Lucy and then back to Hazel. "Can you please tell Mr. Gleason that we'll have to reschedule—"

"No. Hazel, please tell Mr. Gleason we'll be there."

"But, darlin', you're hurt. We can reschedule. They'll understand."

"We're going back to life as usual. Besides we've rescheduled that dinner too many times already. Please relay the message, Hazel."

"Yes, ma'am."

Cal closed the door. "I don't know about you, but I'm not up to playing chase with the Gleasons on a good day, let alone the day after you were nearly killed." He knew his tone had an edge to it, but goddamn it. He'd almost lost her.

Poppy's head came off Lucy's shoulder, and she frowned up at Cal.

"I'm all right, Cal."

"Maybe *you* are."

"I don't know what happened with that article and Priscilla Barnes, but I have a feeling you somehow fixed it. I still have a job to do for you that includes schmoozing that pervy businessman into selling you his business. And I'm betting he called to confirm just so he and Anne can get all of the juicy details about what happened today straight from the horse's mouth. We're going to use that to your advantage."

"Darlin', I couldn't give three shits about what that asshole and his wife want right now. And I'm sure as hell not going to parade you around in front of them so that they can have the freshest, most accurate gossip to share with their friends."

"There's already been so much gossip about us. Wouldn't it be nice if some of it was accurate for a change?"

He let out a frustrated growl. "You're injured."

"I'm fine. Let me do this for you."

"No."

"Cal...please. I want to."

"Stop looking at me like that. Both you and Poppy give me that same look. I'm outnumbered here."

"What look?"

"*That* look. I can't resist you when you look at me like that."

"Then it's settled. Dinner tomorrow night at six with the Gleasons."

11

———

Lucy made Cal go into the office the next morning, wanting everything to go back to normal. Their new normal. The normal they should've had all along. She knew Cal didn't understand why she wanted to keep their dinner plans with the Gleasons, but she refused to let their lives be dictated by Kevin, even in his death. It would be back to the business of living *their* lives.

Besides, she had a pregnancy test to buy and take. She didn't want Cal around for that just in case it came back negative. There was no need to give him another reason to worry about her unless it was absolutely necessary. She thought she'd been nervous taking the pregnancy test when she got pregnant with Poppy, but this was a whole new level of nervousness. So much was riding on this test. A small part of her wished for a negative result. They'd been through so much and had barely started their lives together as a married couple. Did they really need the added stress of having another child so soon? Wouldn't it be better to wait until they decided they were ready?

She had Sam drive her to the store and wait in the car with Poppy. She really shouldn't have been out. The doctors had diagnosed her with a mild concussion, and she had a big bruise on her shoulder from when she had hit the edge of the sink. She was lucky considering what could've happened.

As soon as she got home, she went straight to their bathroom upstairs to take the pregnancy test. Locking the door behind her, she stared at the box in her hand. She read the directions twice to make she sure she didn't do it wrong. Pee on the stick. Wait three minutes. Seemed pretty simple, except there wasn't anything simple about whatever the results would be.

Three minutes was a long time.

She thought back to that first moment when she turned and saw Kevin in the bathroom... It was as though she'd been hurdled back in time to when she'd lived with him and the horrible things he'd done to her. Not just the physical damage. Bruises and cuts healed, pain faded. No, it was the way he got inside her head, the way he twisted everything so she didn't know which side was up. He'd thrown her into a mental pit of despair she didn't think she'd ever be able to climb out of let alone recover from.

The darkness of being so alone, so totally and completely wrong about Kevin when she'd first met him, crawled over her like a fungus, coating her from the inside out. It chewed away tiny bits of her until all that was left was the thin and holey fabric of the person she'd once been. Where she'd gotten the strength to leave, she'd never know. She couldn't even pinpoint the one thing he'd done that had drawn the line for her. One day she got up and got out. Walked right out of the house when she'd been so terrified to go anywhere without him or without his permission.

Maybe it was that something that had made her leave that had also made her stand up to him in that bathroom and fight back. She wished she could say she felt good about killing Kevin. Mostly she just felt sick. And sad. The sadness surprised her. Of all of the emotions she'd thought she'd feel when she was finally free of him, sorrow had to have been the very last, if it was even in the mix at all. Why should she grieve for him? He didn't deserve to be mourned.

She was furious with herself for wasting sorrow on a man who hadn't given her a thought unless it was how to torture her in new and continuously inventive ways. If he were here now, he'd laugh at her stupidity. She'd been *so* stupid where men were concerned. Cal included. She'd read that situation wrong. Twice.

The first time was in her thinking that she could be the one to change Cal. That somehow her love could change him from a billionaire playboy to a family man. The second time was in not recognizing that he *had* changed. He'd reinvented himself in the time they were apart. She guessed she could say that he'd grown up. Now he was every bit the family man she'd wanted him to be the first time around. But a small part of her still didn't trust that change. She had a feeling that the real test of their relationship was yet to come.

These were her thoughts as she waited for the timer to go off for the pregnancy test. She didn't know what to hope for—a negative result or a positive one. She closed her eyes and tried to imagine it coming back negative. Nothing would really change. But what if it was positive? So much would change. She'd get big and fat. Maybe Cal wouldn't like her pregnant. She hadn't lost all of the weight she'd gained from being pregnant with Poppy, and packing more weight on top of that would make it even harder for her to lose after a second pregnancy.

The stretch marks. And the gas, the bloating. The swelling. She'd felt like a giant bowling ball with arms and legs the first time around. What if Cal didn't want another baby? He'd seemed open to the prospect during the only discussion they'd ever had on the subject. There was a big difference between the possibility of a baby versus the reality of one.

At the sound of the ding, she hesitated. Her fate lay in the absence or presence of one tiny blue line. She crept over to where she'd left the test on the counter, took a deep breath, and looked down.

CAL HUNG up the phone and stared off at nothing. Lucas had asked the question that had been hovering at the back of Cal's mind for months. How had Walker known when and where Lucy would be? He'd been ahead of them at every turn. The gun shop. The ball. The party. He knew where to be far enough in advance that he set that fire in the hotel. He'd dressed as one of catering staff at the party at the station. Someone had been tipping him off. There was only one person who knew exactly where Cal would be and when.

Felicia.

It wasn't enough that she'd bugged his office. She'd used her knowledge of his schedule to tip off Walker so he could get to Lucy. It was all he could do to stay in his seat and not go out to Felicia's desk and confront her. He could kill her for what she'd put Lucy through. She'd helped a potential murderer find his victim. Lucy could be dead right now because of what Felicia had done.

He got up and paced, trying to work off some of the murderous rage he felt. There was no way to prove any of it. He had nothing except the bug to hang on her. Unless he got her to confess to what she'd done, there was no way to confirm her involvement. The longer he paced, the more solid his plan became. He knew exactly how he'd trap her—by using her attraction to him. It was the only motivation she had for doing what she'd done. So he'd use it against her.

He went over to his desk and pressed the intercom. "Felicia?"

"Yes, Mr. Sellers?"

"Can you come into my office please?"

"Yes, sir."

He set the cameras in his office to record their conversation, then leaned back against his desk, placing his hands on either side of him, and tried to look casual. He could do this. He could make her believe he was into her to get her to confess. This was for Lucy.

Felicia came in with her tablet, prepared to take notes as she always did, and sat in one of the chairs. She pushed her arms together so that her breasts lifted, trying to get him to notice her. "What can I do for you, sir?"

"How long have we worked together, Felicia?"

"Almost two years."

"In that time have I ever told you how much I appreciate your hard work and dedication?"

"Well...no."

"I do. I want you to know that. I've recently realized some things about my life and the people in it."

She slid forward in her seat.

"You're one of the few people who I feel like I can really trust," he said. "You've become an important part of my business...and my life. Thank you."

She set her tablet on the chair and stood. "It's my pleasure, sir." She put a little extra sway in her hips as she closed the distance between them until they were mere inches apart. "I mean that. I'd do anything for you."

"I know you would. And I can't tell you how much that means to me."

Running a finger along his jaw, she leaned in so that she was between his thighs. He could smell her perfume —something heavy and cloying. "You're one of the most handsome and powerful men I've ever known. So sexy."

"I'm glad you think so." He gripped her finger and held it between them. "You said you'd do anything for me. What exactly would you do?"

"Anything you want."

"I'm a married man. That doesn't bother you?"

"Why should it? You can't be happy. I mean, I get that she had your baby, but she's also brought you a lot of problems."

"And if I wanted to be rid of her...that's something you'd do for me?"

"In a minute. You don't even have to ask. In fact..." She wrapped her arms around his neck. "I've been working on that problem. I know how unhappy you've been. I see it on you every day. So I did a little digging."

"That's very perceptive of you." He put his hands on her waist and drew her in closer. Touching her made him sick. She didn't feel like Lucy or smell like Lucy. She didn't do anything for him except disgust him. "What did you find out?"

"I'm very disappointed in you."

"In what way?"

She moved away. He followed, hoping to get what he needed out of her.

Standing behind his desk, she ran a finger over one of the business awards he'd received. "I've always admired your business sense. You've always seemed so smart and capable. Except where she was concerned. What is it about her that makes you lose all perspective?" She whirled on him, her eyes narrowed. "What is she holding over your head? What is it she has that I don't?"

"We have a history together, a daughter." And so, so much more. He tamped all of that down to do what needed to be done. If she saw his true feelings for Lucy, she'd know this scene for the charade it was.

She wandered around the other side of the desk, her hips swaying. He stuck close to her. She glanced back at him, a sly smirk on her face. She liked him chasing her. If that's what it took to get her to confess, he'd follow her wherever she went until she told him what he needed to hear.

"Her husband stopped by here one day while you were out." She leaned back against the desk in a seductive pose. "He was very anxious to know where she was."

"You wicked, wicked girl, keeping secrets from me."

She grabbed his tie and pulled. He stumbled into her, catching himself on the desk so he didn't tumble her down across it. She wrapped his tie around her hand, and he could tell she liked pushing him around. It turned her on. He'd play her game.

"I was hoping he could convince her that they belonged together." She pulled him closer and whispered, "The way you and I belong together."

Just a few more minutes...

"Do you think we belong together, sir?"

"I want you to call me Cal."

"No. I like calling you sir."

He spoke next to her ear. "So damn sexy."

She pushed him away from her, still gripping his tie. "You didn't answer my question—do you think we belong together?"

"Without a doubt."

She yanked him close again. "I'm so glad to hear you say that."

Sliding her leg up his, she caught the back of his knees. He lost his balance, grabbing her to keep from taking them both down.

"I'd do anything for you, *sir*, anything to make you mine."

Closing his eyes, he pretended she was someone else —anyone else—and pitched his voice low, seductive. "Tell me what you'd do."

"I'll help you, but first tell me what you would do...for me...to me."

"Whatever you want. What is it you want, Felicia?"

"Call me honey the way you used to before *her*."

"What do you want, honey?"

"I want you all to myself."

"You said you didn't mind that I was married."

"I lied." She licked along his jaw, her breath hot in his ear. "I won't share you. I'm going to be the only one you fuck." She jerked on his tie. "Got it?"

"Yes, honey."

"It wasn't very smart of you to marry Lucy without a prenup. I'm very disappointed in you for that. A divorce would cost you a fortune."

"I wasn't thinking. My daughter—"

"Now it makes sense." She pushed him away again, his tie still in her grip.

She liked the power play, got off on it. He'd give her what she wanted to get what he wanted.

Licking her upper lip, she ran her gaze over him. "She has you by the balls." She moved fast, cupping his junk.

He grabbed her wrist and twisted, forcing her to let go of him, and brought her hand to his chest where he could control it. Son of a bitch, this woman was a piece of work.

"Something like that," he answered, trying real hard to remember he was supposed to be letting her seduce him.

"Hmm. I was hoping her ex-husband would take care of your little problem, but unfortunately she killed him, ruining all of my plans and hard work."

"You were willing to do that...for me?"

"I told you. I'd do anything for you."

He stroked the inside of her wrist. "What was your plan?"

"It was rather clever really. I'd tell him where she'd be, gave him the security codes or whatever he needed, and he was supposed to convince her to go away with him. He was either too stupid or he overestimated Lucy's desire to be a rich man's wife. But I'm not like her. I don't care about your money. All I want is you."

She jerked on his tie, at the same time wrapping her legs around him, knocking him off balance. He landed on top of her on the desk, her mouth fastened to his.

"Oh, my God."

Lucy.

He shoved at Felicia and rolled off her to find Lucy standing in the doorway, one hand over mouth, the other fisted over her belly.

"It's not what it looks like," he said.

"It's exactly what it looks like." Felicia pressed herself against him and ran a hand up his chest, making a grab for his tie, but he caught it and flung it away.

He moved toward his wife. "Lucy, you've got to believe me."

Lucy shook her head. "I'm such an idiot. I can't believe I trusted you. Again." She spun on her heels and ran out of his office.

"Lucy!"

He started after her, but Felicia jumped into his path. "Let her go. We can finally be together."

"Shut the fuck up." He pushed past her and ran down the hall. The elevator doors closed before he could hit the button and call it back. "Goddamn it!"

He bolted for the stairs, running for his life. The look on her face—exactly the same expression she had the last time she caught him—shock, pain, and then hatred. He'd never forget that look, he'd never get out from under it. He would always be the man who broke her in two. She'd told him that if he ever cheated on her again, they'd be over. Really over. The fact that he hadn't cheated this time meant nothing up against the visual of him lying on top of Felicia on his desk.

He had to find her, had to somehow make her see that what she'd witnessed in his office wasn't the truth. He wasn't that man anymore. He hadn't betrayed her.

By the time he got to the lobby, Lucy was climbing into the car with Sam. They drove off before he could stop them. He raised his hand and flagged down a cab. Climbing in, he gave the driver directions to follow Sam's car. He called Lucy, but she didn't answer so he tried Sam.

"Hello?"

"Sam, it's Cal. Let me talk to Lucy."

There was some muffled mumbling and then Sam came back on the line. "She doesn't want to talk to you."

"Put me on speakerphone."

He could hear Sam asking Lucy if she wanted to hear what Cal had to say. And then Lucy's emphatic "No."

"Tell her that Felicia was the one who was helping Walker get to Lucy."

"I don't think that's going to help your case, man."

"I was getting Felicia's confession when Lucy walked in."

More mumbling.

"She says that's exactly what it looked like to her— taking down a confession."

"Damn it, Sam! I'm not having an affair with Felicia."

"She's crying," Sam whispered. "I'm sorry. I'm going to have to hang up now."

"Goddamn it!"

The driver glanced at him in the rearview mirror. "Lady troubles?"

"Yeah."

The driver pointed at his lips. "You got some lipstick... You should probably wipe that off before we catch up to that car."

Cal swiped a hand across his mouth. The pink of Felicia's lipstick streaked his skin, a damning reminder of what an idiot he was and how big a task he had ahead of him. "Shit."

~

LUCY COULDN'T BELIEVE how stupid she was. Almost two years later and she was right back where she'd ended things with Cal the first time. She'd taken a chance on surprising him at his office to invite him out to lunch. Things with them had felt off kilter, and she thought maybe spending some time together might help. She'd planned for Sam to wait for her with Poppy just in case Cal wasn't available. It was a good thing. Otherwise she'd be having her breakdown in the back of a taxi.

"I'm sorry, Lucy." Sam patted her hand in her lap. "Men can be real assholes sometimes."

"I can't believe I trusted him again. I'm such an idiot. What am I supposed to do now?"

"Now you go home and have a good long cry and then you think about what you want to do."

"I can't. It's not my home, it's Cal's."

"I know you don't want to hear this right now, but is it possible you could've misinterpreted what happened back there?"

"Well, I don't know. If you walked into your wife's office and she had her secretary on his back on her desk and was on top of him, kissing him, what impression would you get?"

"It's just that I've seen the way he looks at you, and I can't see him looking at any other woman that way."

"He was doing a lot more than looking at another woman just now. This isn't the first time I caught him cheating on me, Sam." Putting her hands over her face, she collapsed forward. "What am I going to do?"

She had nowhere to go and no money that wasn't Cal's. She was homeless with a child to support. Things couldn't possibly get any worse.

"I don't even know where to tell you to take us." She swiped at the tears that wouldn't stop falling. "I don't have any money for a hotel room. There's no way I'd ever go back to my mother's house."

"I'm taking you home."

"I don't have a home anymore!" Her outburst woke up Poppy, who'd been asleep in the backseat. "I'm sorry, sweetie. Sshhh. It's all right." Lucy handed her daughter her favorite stuffed animal and noticed a taxi behind them with a familiar outline in the backseat. "How long has that taxi been following us?"

"Since we left Cal's building."

"That son of a bitch! Pull over."

"What?"

"Pull over."

"We're on the highway."

"Sam, if you don't pull this car over, I'm going to grab the wheel myself."

"All right, all right." Sam maneuvered the car to the side of the road and stopped.

Just as Lucy predicted, the taxi pulled up behind them. She opened her door and marched toward the other car.

Cal climbed out of the back and stood with the door open. "Darlin', you have to believe me. Nothing happened back there."

"I don't have to do shit where you're concerned, Cal Sellers. I told you that if you ever cheated on me, we were through. We're officially through, you lying, no good, dick-for-brains cheat!"

Cal slammed the car door and stalked toward her. "I didn't cheat!"

Lucy parked her hands on her hips. "Really? 'Cause where I'm from, crawling between the legs of your *honey* on top of your desk is cheating!"

They were feet apart now, yelling and gesturing at each other. Traffic slowed to watch.

"She attacked me. I swear to God, darlin'—"

"Don't call me darlin'! Don't call me anything ever again."

"There isn't another woman in this world I want more that you. I swear it. If you'll just listen to me—"

"Listening to you got me in this predicament in the first place. Listening to you is how I wound up in the exact same position as I was in two years ago. Listening to you is how I got my heart broken by you twice. I can't listen to you anymore, Cal. I can't afford your words. They cost me too much."

His voice softened to where she could barely hear it. "Dar—Lucy, I'm so sorry you're hurting because of me, but I swear to you—"

"You can swear out a formal statement in blood and I wouldn't believe a word of it." She threw her hands up. "I can't believe I've been such an idiot where you're concerned."

He started to take a step toward her, but she put a hand up to stop him. Seeing him now churned up every single emotion she had inside her. But the one that beat the others to the front was anger. She was so damned angry with him, with herself, and with the whole damn mess she was in. Before she knew what she meant to do, she hauled off and slapped him in the face. It was like something let loose inside her, and she went blind with rage, beating ineffectually at him until she was nearly out of breath and he caught her wrists.

He put his face close to hers, his eyes pleading every bit as much as his words. "Lucy, she's the one who was working with your ex. That's how he knew where you'd be and when. That's what I was doing with her before things got out of hand—getting her to admit it. On tape. I swear it. Please. You have to believe me."

She stopped trying to break free and stared at him, wondering how she'd gotten here. How had her life done a complete one-eighty, landing her right back where she'd last left off with him? And the thing of it was she *wanted* to believe him. She wanted him to prove to her that he hadn't betrayed her again, that she wasn't a fool to have trusted him a second time.

"Come back to the office with me. I'll show you. Please, Lucy."

Could this be true? Could he be telling the truth?

12

C al was literally fighting for his family and his life with Lucy on the side of a highway with people slowing to take photos and video. She was furious with him. He could hardly blame her. He'd let things with Felicia get out of hand. He was only now realizing what a completely stupid idea it had been to try to seduce a confession out of her. Of course Lucy had walked in. That was his dumb luck. The look on her face...just like the last time she'd caught him with his assistant on top of his desk. Lucy was right. He did have a dick for brains.

"Come back to the office with me," he pleaded. "I recorded the whole thing. Come and watch the tape. You'll see I'm telling you the truth. I love you so much. I don't know what I'd do without you. Please. Please believe me."

"*She* told Kevin where I'd be?"

"Yes." He could tell his words were having some effect on her. She was starting to believe him. "She gave him the code to our security gate. That's how he got in with the flowers. She told him about the shooting range, the ball, and the party at the studio. She knew exactly where we'd be and when. I started to get suspicious of her after your interview with Priscilla Barnes. Felicia had to have been the one to feed her that info about our arrangement. She was in the outer office while you were in my office. She must've listened in. Don't you see?"

Lucy looked off past Cal. She was thinking now instead of reacting out of emotion. He could see it in the way her brow furrowed and her lips pressed together.

"I want to see this supposed tape you have," she said.

All the air left Cal's body, and he nearly dropped to his knees. She believed him. Or at the very least she was entertaining the idea of believing him. All he had to do was get her back to his office and show her the tape.

"Stay right there. Don't move. Let me pay my cab fare, and I'll ride back with you."

"No. I'll meet you there."

"Okay. That works too." He looked up at the news helicopter that circled above and around the traffic jam they were causing. Their scene would likely make the local news. For some reason he didn't care.

She started to walk back to the car.

"Lucy?"

She stopped but didn't turn.

"I love you, darlin', more than anything. Please know that."

She resumed walking to the car and climbed in. He ran back to the cab and jumped inside.

"We still following that car?" the cabbie asked.

"Yes. We're going back the way we came."

The driver glanced up at the circling helicopter through the windshield and then stuck his head and arm out of his window and waved. "I'm going to be on TV."

"Just go. Don't lose sight of that car."

It took them an extra fifteen minutes to get back to Cal's office building, and it cost him a fortune for the cab ride, but it was worth it. Lucy would see that he was telling the truth, and everything would go back to normal. A new normal now that her asshole ex was lying in the morgue. A better normal.

"What are you smiling at?" Lucy asked as he held the front door of his building open for her.

"I'm looking forward to taking you home after this and celebrating our new normal without Walker, without extra security. That's all."

"You're awfully confident this tape will prove you're not lying, aren't you?"

"As confident as a man with one foot over the finish line."

Except he still wasn't all that confident where she was concerned. He'd fucked up before and she'd taken him back. Things might not turn out that way a second time. She'd trusted him enough on the side of that freeway to give him the opportunity to prove he wasn't the cheating bastard she thought he was. He wouldn't take a full breath until she saw the tape and believed him.

They rode the elevator in silence. He kept stealing glances at her. She was so damn beautiful with her hair fluffed out from the wind and her cheeks red from her anger. If she wasn't so boiling mad at him, he'd be thinking about putting more flush in her cheeks. To keep himself from touching her, he put his hands behind his back.

They exited the elevator, and he hurried ahead to

open his office door for her. They both ignored the stares of the employees who had no doubt gotten quite a show with both of them tearing out of there, then coolly strolling back in.

He closed the door and went straight for the control panel behind his desk. The system was off. It should've still been on from when he'd set it up before confronting Felicia.

"Oh, shit. *No.*"

He flipped some switches and waited for the monitor to come to life. Gone. The whole scene was gone. Felicia must've seen that he'd had it on when she went behind his desk. That was why she'd jumped him. She must've planned to confront Lucy with the tape. But then Lucy had come in and he'd blown the whole thing by chasing after her. Felicia had to have known his plan then and deleted the tape because it incriminated *her.*

He sat down hard in his seat, fully aware that Lucy was standing a few feet away, waiting for him to prove something he had absolutely no proof of. He was totally fucked.

"It's gone." He turned to face her. "Felicia must've deleted it off the system after we left."

"Right."

"I swear..." He had no more fight in him. All he had to rely on was her trust, which he knew he hadn't fully earned back yet. "I swear to you I'm telling the truth."

There it was. All of it laid out before her for her to decide—their present and their future. If she didn't believe him, there was nothing left between them. The one thing she'd asked of him was to not cheat on her again, and in her eyes that was exactly what he'd done. He'd promised her, and he'd screwed it up.

"I told you that I could take anything, Cal, anything except you cheating on me. Then I walk in on you with your secretary *again*. And then you humiliate me by dragging me back in here to do what? Try to convince me that what I saw wasn't what I saw? You had your hands on her. You were kissing her."

"That's not what—"

"Don't tell me that's not what happened! I saw it with my own damn eyes. And the night you came home with lipstick on your face and you said it was Anne Gleason's, that was really Felicia's lipstick, wasn't it? How long have you and Felicia been sleeping together? From the beginning?"

"No. I've never done anything with Felicia. What I told you that night was the truth. It was Anne Gleason's lipstick." He could see it all through her eyes, all of the things that stacked up against him and chipped away at her trust.

"So you just go about your day and women throw themselves at you left and right. You're completely innocent."

"Yes."

She folded her arms across her chest. "How many?"

"What?"

"How many women have there been, Cal? All of those late nights at work, those last-minute out-of-town meetings. And I bought into it all, believing everything that came pouring out of your mouth."

"That *was* all business. There is only you. There's only ever been you. I swear it." He could tell she didn't believe him. The more he denied it the less she believed. He wanted to go to her and put his arms around her and tell her he didn't even look at other women, that she was it for him. If she left him, there would be no other.

She stood in front of his desk, her eyes dry, her back straight, staring at him like she couldn't believe what was happening.

"I'm pregnant." She laughed as though it was some kind of joke and she was the butt of it. "I'm pregnant and alone. Again."

Her words ripped through him, breaking open everything inside him. She was pregnant. His mind cataloged the information and spun its wheels trying to process it. He could only stare at her in disbelief. He'd worked like a damned dog to earn back her trust only to wind up where they'd left off the first time. He'd hurt her bad before, but this time there would be no second chance. There would be no reconciliation.

She'd have his child without him. He'd be there just outside the room, writing checks and making sure she got what she needed, but he wouldn't see his child come into the world. She'd go it alone, taking nothing from him, wanting nothing to do with him. He'd have to stand at the back of another church and watch her pledge herself to another man. And there wasn't a damn thing he could do about it.

Again.

She turned and walked out of his office. And his life.

It took everything inside of Lucy to stride out of Cal's office as though nothing was wrong when *everything* was wrong. He honestly thought she'd buy that crap about a tape. That he'd get her alone, do more of his swearing to the truth and double-talking, and she'd fall right back in line. Hell, if he'd kissed her in the elevator like she knew he'd wanted to do, she might've caved. She was that weak where he was concerned.

At least that bitch Felicia had the good sense to leave, or Lucy would've had to walk past the woman who'd destroyed her marriage. She made it just inside the elevator before breaking down. She'd told him she was pregnant and he'd sat there. No expression change at all. No elation. No disappointment. Nothing. She was carrying his child. And she was well and truly alone.

The past might've partially repeated itself, but she was going to make damn sure it didn't fully repeat. She wouldn't turn to the first man who would have her like she'd done with Kevin. She'd find a way to make it as a single mother of two children.

Goddamn Cal and his goddamned knack for making her believe in him then knocking her on her ass. The only way things could get worse was if she was carrying twins. She laughed out loud at the possibility, knowing she looked like a lunatic crossing the lobby with tears streaming down her cheeks. It would be her luck to not only get knocked up by the same lowlife, cheating scum— twice—but to get knocked up the second time with twins. Twins.

Sam got out of the car when he saw her and came around to open the door for her. "No tape?"

"No tape."

"Ah, damn. I'm sorry, Lucy. Are you sure about this?"

Nodding, she climbed into the car and stared straight ahead. What was she going to do? Where was she going to go?

Sam's cell phone rang. He glanced at the display then answered it. "Sam here." He listened for a few moments. "All right. I'll tell her. Yeah. I'm sorry. Bye." He hit the End button. "Cal says to take you home. He'll stay somewhere else. He says the house is yours and Poppy's. The staff and I will stay on with you. That's what he wants."

"You know what I want, Sam? I want a husband who doesn't fuck his secretaries. That's what I want. When do I get what I want? Hmm?" She put up a hand. "Don't answer. It was a rhetorical question. I'm not accepting his home and his employees. Or his guilt. Please drop me and Poppy off at Mi and Lucas's."

"I'll stay with you."

"No offense, Sam, but you're fired. I can't afford to pay you. Besides, we don't need a ninja nanny anymore."

"But Cal—"

"Say his name one more time and I'll get me and Poppy out of this car, and we'll walk to their house."

"Yes, ma'am."

She had no plan other than to get through the next few hours. Sam insisted on going up to Mi and Lucas's apartment with her. She caught sight of herself in the mirrored elevator doors to their apartment and nearly gasped. Her hair practically stood on end, and her eyes were red and swollen. If they didn't take her in, she had no other options. How could they refuse her looking so pitiful with Poppy on her hip and nothing but what was in the diaper bag and her purse to call her own?

The front desk had announced them and sent them up in the elevator, so Mi and Lucas were waiting for them when it opened into their apartment.

"Lucy." Mi's voice was full of sympathy as she scooped her and Poppy into a hard hug.

Mi's big pregnant belly made it difficult to get very close. The thought that soon Lucy would be as big as Mi made her burst into tears all over again.

"Oh, sweetie. Come in and sit down." Mi guided Lucy into the living room and down onto the couch. "Here, let me take her." Mi held her hands out for Poppy.

Lucy handed her over and watched as Mi tried to settle the baby on what was left of her lap. "I'm sorry to barge in on you like this." Lucy swiped at the tears that wouldn't stop falling. "If I had somewhere else to go..."

"I'm glad you came here. What happened? Is Cal all right?"

"Oh, Cal's just *fine*."

Lucy filled Mi in on what had happened between her and Cal, right down to the humiliating scene in his office when he admitted there was no tape. The image of Cal on top of Felicia with his mouth on hers played over and over in a loop through Lucy's head. She couldn't get the picture of him standing next to his desk, his hair rumpled with lipstick on his lips, out of her mind either. What had made him think bringing her back to the scene of his crimes would help him convince her she'd imagined the whole thing?

"That son of a bitch," Mi breathed. "I can't believe he did that to you. Twice."

"I can't either. And I can't believe I fell for him and his lies all over again. And that's not even the worst part... I'm pregnant. Oh, my God, Mi, what am I going to do?"

"You're going to stay here as long as you need to. We'll help you get back on your feet."

"I can't put you out. You're about to have a baby of your own."

"You're not putting us out. We have plenty of room. Or if you'd rather have a place of your own, the tenants in my old house moved out last month. We've been working on getting it ready to rent out again. It's yours if you want it."

"You're way too good to me. Thank you for not saying I told you so. Because you did, the day we got married."

"I did?"

"You asked me if I was sure I wanted to marry him. At the time I didn't have any other choice. I had to protect Poppy, but now... I need to stop making decisions out of desperation where men are concerned. I need to be alone for a while to figure things out. Thank you for your generous offer."

"What about the baby and Poppy?"

"They'll be with me."

"What about their father? I've seen him with Poppy, and I can't imagine he'll give them up."

"I really don't care what he does or doesn't do right now. Right now I just want this day to end. I don't want to be in the day my life imploded anymore."

"Come with me." Mi took Lucy's hand and led her into one of their guestrooms. "This will be your room as long as you need it. Why don't you lie down and take a nap?"

"What about Poppy?"

Mi held Poppy to her. "She'll be good practice for Lucas and me. Go on, get some rest. Things won't seem so bleak when you wake up, I promise."

"I doubt that. I'll still be a single mother with another child on the way when I wake up."

Mi helped her get into bed and pulled the covers over her. She held Poppy so Lucy could give her a kiss. "Now get some rest."

～

CAL HAD RECEIVED some good news on a night that was far from good. Gleason had finally agreed to sell him his company. Sellers Investments was saved. He wasn't sure what he'd said to Joel to get him to relent. He'd called to cancel dinner yet again. Joel had asked him if he needed anything, no doubt having heard all about his and Lucy's scene on the side of the freeway. Too far from caring what happened next, Cal had pathetically joked that he needed Joel to sell him Gleason Investments. There was silence and then by some miracle Joel had agreed. Just like that.

Closeted in his darkened office, he was now halfway to drunk. All evening long he'd sat with his phone in his hand, bringing up Lucy's number, then exiting the screen before placing the call. He knocked back the last swallow of whiskey and hurled the glass on an anguished roar. It hit the wall and shattered, raining shards across the carpet. That glass was fucking frustrating and deserved to die for being empty too goddamned soon. He'd clean it up in the morning. Right now he kind of liked the metaphor of the chunks of glass scattered across the floor like the pieces of his life—too sharp and painful to pick up and do anything with.

He'd been an idiot. Right from the start. Proposing marriage to her... He let out a merciless chuckle and took a swig straight from the whiskey bottle. What a fucking joke. He should've offered her a position in one of his other divisions. But he'd been selfish, wanting her back with everything in him, so he'd suggested marriage instead of what she'd really needed—a job and a loan to help her get back on her feet.

Then he'd gone about trying to bed her. What a clusterfuck that had been. Again he'd only thought of himself and what he wanted. She'd been broken and battered, but he was going to somehow fix her with orgasms and his magic cock. He'd helped her, all right, by taking the single greatest thing she'd given him besides their daughter—her trust—and shit all over it by using Felicia's attraction to him to get her to confess.

What a self-centered asshole he was.

Her words and hollow laugh looped through his head over and over. She was pregnant. He wouldn't get a second chance to experience any of the things he'd missed with Poppy like doctor appointments, ultrasounds, and seeing his child take its first steps.

And again he was only thinking of himself and how he was affected.

Because she was so proud and stubborn she'd made herself homeless, jobless, and penniless. She'd rather go through everything alone than take one single thing from him. He could hardly blame her. All he'd ever given her was pain, pain, and more pain. Anything he offered her would be a pale comparison to what she needed.

The whiskey wasn't working fast enough. He put the bottle to his lips and tilted his head back to take a good, long draw off it. He set it down with a thunk and blinked. At first he wasn't sure what he was seeing. The weak light from his desk lamp didn't quite make it to the doorway. He'd thought for a moment it might be Lucy, and his heart jackhammered.

The proportions were all wrong. Not Lucy. Hazel? No, not Hazel.

"Hello, Cal."

Motherfucking Felicia.

How had she gotten in? Oh, fuck, that's right. He'd forgotten to change the gate code and tell Hazel he'd fired Felicia. Except he hadn't fired her. Yet.

"You tried to trick me." She closed the door and moved closer into the glow of the desk lamp.

She looked perfect just like she did every day she came to work. He'd hired her partly for her experience as an executive assistant and mainly for her looks. Not that he'd been interested in her. He'd built an image of himself that for some reason he'd felt the need to perpetuate. But now—staring at her past the barrel of her gun—those reasons seemed completely stupid and childish.

"Hands on the desk," she ordered.

The alcohol and the shock had made him slow to react, too slow to press the silent alarm before he had to follow her command.

"Did you think I didn't know what you were doing? I know you, Cal. I know you better than you know yourself. I know everything about you."

"Not everything."

"No?"

"No," he answered. "And by the way, you're fired."

She tilted her head to one side and considered him for a moment. "You're drunk."

"Not drunk enough. What's the gun for?"

"In case you do something stupid like you did in your office." She wagged a finger at him. "That was naughty of you to tape our...encounter. Too bad your hysterical wife came in and ruined everything." She took in the room. "Do you have cameras in here too?"

He couldn't wrap his head around what she wanted or why she was here. She stood there steady-handed and calm, wanting what?

"Yes."

"Are they on right now?" she asked.

"No."

"That's too bad."

"What do you want, Felicia?"

"I want you, but I don't think you want me, and that's a problem. I didn't like that game you tried to play with me in your office, pretending to be interested in me so you could get me to confess. Do you have any idea the things I've done for you? And that's the way you thank me." She shook her head and made a tsking sound. "You're lucky I didn't have my gun with me this afternoon."

"Why are you here?"

"I'm here to make sure *she's* gone. You see, with her out of the way it's just a matter of time before you love me as much as I love you. I love you so much. I don't think you really understand how much. Or the things I'd do to have you. So I'm going to tie you up and take care of her. Permanently. And then I'm going to come back here and see what fun we can have with you tied up and the cameras on."

"She's not here." And thank God for that. "She left me. Because of you."

"She is one dumb bitch to give you up just like that." She snapped her fingers. "What in the hell did you see in her?"

"Everything. I love her."

She reached into the duffle bag strapped across her chest and pulled out a pair of handcuffs. "Put these on." She tossed him the cuffs. He let them skid across the desk and onto the floor. "Pick them up!"

"No."

She rushed forward and pointed the gun inches from his face. "I *said* to pick them up and put them on."

He made his move, grabbing for the gun and pushing it left while twisting his body to the right. She landed on him, knocking him back in the chair. They hit the floor hard with her still on top. His head struck the floor with the brunt of both of their weight. The air rushed out of him, and light flashed at the back of his eyes. She used his momentary loss of control to her advantage, bringing her knee up to his groin. He shifted, and she caught him in the side of the thigh, barely missing his nuts.

She came at his face with her nails, raking them across his eyes and cheeks. He grasped her wrist. Grappling with her, he tried to get control of the gun. But she was too strong and he was too drunk.

BAM!

13

Lucy lay there in the big comfy bed, her head pounding, her eyes itchy and swollen, praying for sleep. But all she did was miss Cal and his big body lying next to hers. She thought about never being held by him, or kissed by him, or loved by him ever again. The pain spread through her, filling every inch to the point where she physically ached. This time was worse than the last. This time she'd invested more and loved him more. He'd been everything, and now she had to make him nothing.

After tossing and turning for what felt like forever, she got up and went to the window. It was dark outside. She hadn't thought it had been that long since she'd lain down. Poppy. She needed to go check on her baby girl. Creeping out into the hall, she wasn't sure which room Mi could've put Poppy in. Maybe the nursery? The door was ajar, so she quietly pushed it open.

Sam was asleep on the daybed next to the crib where Poppy slept. Damn that man. She had no way to pay him, and he knew it. She'd fired him, but there he was still caring for and guarding her daughter. If there was one hero in all this mess, it was Sam. God bless him. He was more reliable and trustworthy than her own damn husband. And that was a sad state of affairs, if she trusted her nanny more than her child's father.

She tiptoed back out of the room and headed toward the living room. The bluish light at the other end of the hall let her know that someone was up, watching TV. She hoped it was Mi, but as she came into the room those hopes were quickly dashed as she saw Lucas's large frame on the sofa, backlit by the television. She hadn't spent much time alone with the big man her friend had married and felt kind of awkward about disturbing him, so she turned to go back the way she'd come.

"Can't sleep, Lucy?" Lucas asked.

How'd he know it was her?

"These days Mi moans with practically every step she takes."

And psychic too? "Sorry. I didn't mean to disturb you."

He shifted to look at her. "You're not. I'm not much of a sleeper. Maybe we can find an old movie to watch or something."

"Sure." She made her way over and curled up in an overstuffed chair next to the couch. "What's on?"

"What do you like to watch?"

"I really don't care."

Lucas flicked through the channels slowly. "Let me know when something catches your eye."

"Thanks for letting me stay here. I know we sort of crashed in on you. And thanks for letting Sam stay. He should've left. I fired him."

"Why'd you fire him?"

"I can't afford him."

"But Cal—"

"I'm not taking anything from that man. So don't even say it."

"He takes care of what's his, so you're going to have a tough time making that stick."

She let out a frustrated breath. "I swear to God if one more person tries to reason me into accepting so much as a stick of gum from that no good son of a bitch, I'm going to scream. He's taken care of things all right. He's taken great care to totally fuck up my life...again. Did Mi tell you that I'm pregnant?"

"She mentioned it. Congratulations? I'm sorry?"

"That pretty much covers it."

"I've known Cal a long time—"

"I don't need the sales pitch. I've already bought."

Lucas laughed. "I get it. I won't mention Cal again except to say that he's texted me about eighty times to check in on you and Poppy. And I know you're not going to like it, but you're stuck with Sam. He's been ordered not to leave you."

"Ordered. Of all the arrogant— Wait. Go back a couple of channels."

Lucas clicked back to a local news station.

"That's my house." She shook her head. "I mean Cal's house. What in the hell is going on? Turn it up."

"Local authorities were called to infamous Dallas businessman Cal Sellers's home just after nine o'clock this evening when the silent alarm was triggered by a bullet piercing a lower floor window. Apparently Mr. Sellers's former assistant, a Felicia McAdams who has been taken into police custody, broke into his home and shot at him. Along with the gun, McAdams brought a duffle bag in which she had rope, tape, handcuffs, and a taser—all of the tools required for a kidnapping. Mr. Sellers was home at the time of the break-in, and we're told he was treated on the scene and released with minor injuries.

"The police have been mum on what the motive might be for this crime, and Mr. Sellers was unavailable for comment." The picture changed to an aerial view of Cal and Lucy yelling at each other on the side of the freeway. "Earlier this afternoon Mr. Sellers and his wife, Lucy Sellers, were filmed having what looks like an argument on the shoulder of the I-35 freeway. Could the two incidents be related? We'll have up-to-the-minute updates on this incident as information comes to us. Back to you in the studio."

Lucas got up and pulled his cell phone out, then went into the other room. Lucy grabbed the remote to try to find more coverage on another channel. Felicia broke into their house? The reporter said Cal had been treated and released, but what if he wasn't okay? What if "unavailable for comment" was code for lying bleeding in the hospital? If Felicia and Cal were having an affair, then why did she break in? Who had she planned on kidnapping? What in the hell was going on?

THE BULLET SMASHED the window above Cal, setting off the security alarm. Glass rained down on them, lodging into his skin as he rolled Felicia and pinned her down. She fought hard, bucking underneath him. Security arrived and it took three of them to subdue her and cuff her hands behind her back with her own handcuffs. The rest was a blur of people coming in and out, poking at him with their questions. His head pounded from the fall to the floor, his face burned, and all he wanted was to see Lucy and Poppy to make sure they were okay. But the police wouldn't let him make any phone calls.

After giving his side of the story to the police, he had to recite it all again for Lucas, who had seen the report on TV. Cal finally got a report on Lucy and Poppy. He'd been terrified that Felicia had gotten to them first before she'd come after him. He was dying to talk to Lucy, but that might only make things worse.

Lucas had said Lucy was okay, but he knew she wasn't. None of them were.

He didn't deserve Lucy. He didn't deserve to have everything that came with being with her, including raising their children. He'd be the weekend dad, the Disneyland dad, always trying to make up for what he'd screwed up.

It didn't matter what Lucy said. He would take care of her. He'd promised her that she and Poppy—and now the baby—would always have a safe place to live, and he meant to keep that promise. She would have Sam as long as she needed him. He'd buy her a new home if she wouldn't take his. He'd be everything he could be to her from the outside. Always on the outside.

He'd never get to hold Lucy again. Never get to dance with her, make love to her, or just lie next to her. He'd never walk into a room and find her there or be greeted by her when he came home. He wouldn't be a part of her pregnancy, and she likely wouldn't want him there when she gave birth. He'd have to wait like a distant relative to find out if it was a boy or a girl. He wouldn't get to decide on a name or hold their child while he or she was still warm from Lucy's body.

He wouldn't get his family back.

He'd just started up the stairs when the doorbell rang again. "Goddamned cops," he mumbled. "Can't you come—" The rest of the sentence died in his throat when he opened the door to find Lucy standing on his doorstep. He blinked. This had to be part of the head injury.

"Oh," she breathed. "Your face."

He put a hand up to his cheek then regretted it when it burned.

"Lucas said you weren't hurt bad, but that looks very painful."

"It burns." He stared at her. Was she real?

"I wanted to see for myself that you were okay. They didn't give very many details on TV, and Lucas gave me even less." She glanced around at the doorway, the frame, the floor... "It's late. I should probably go."

"No!" He put a hand on her shoulder. She *was* real. He pulled his hand right back when she glared down at it. "I mean... Would you like to come in?"

She moved forward without comment. He backed up, giving her room. As soon as she was inside, he closed the door, afraid she'd flitter right back out like a butterfly.

She turned to him in the foyer, her hands clasped behind her back. He couldn't stop looking at her. She didn't have any makeup on, and her eyes were a little puffy, probably from crying, but to him she'd never been more beautiful.

"How's Poppy?" he asked.

"Fine. Sam's with her at Mi and Lucas's."

"That's where you're staying?"

"Lucas or Sam didn't tell you?"

"No. Lucas only gave me the barest details, and all Sam would say was that you and Poppy were safe."

"I'm surprised. I would've thought they'd report every-thing to you."

"I think they're almost as pissed at me as you are."

"Yeah, well..."

"I'm sorry," he blurted out.

"Me too."

"What are you sorry for?"

"I should've seen Felicia for what she was. But when I walked in on you with Felicia, all of those old feelings came back—the humiliation, the anger, the hurt. I couldn't see past that to what was real, and I'm sorry for it."

"You don't have a damn thing to be sorry for. When you laid everything out to me in my office, I knew how it must've looked to you. Add in our history and... I'm sorry. Honest to God, I'm so sorry I put you through all that."

She nodded. "We have some luck, don't we?"

"The worst. Look at you, knocked up by a no-account, dick for brains like me. And look at me—I can't stop fucking up the best thing that ever happened to me."

"Cal, what happened in your office and here tonight?"

"You want the short version or the long version?"

"I want your version."

"Will you come in and sit down?" He waited for her response with the same nervous stomach he'd had when he first started knocking on her bedroom door.

At her nod, he exhaled the breath he'd been holding and led her into their living room like she was a guest. He even offered her a beverage when she was seated. His head throbbed in time with his heart, which beat so hard he thought it might break a rib.

He sat on the sofa next to her, close enough to touch but not to crowd. The whole thing reminded him of the night she'd come to him wet from the rain to tell him that she'd marry him. Only this time around there was more at stake. So much more.

He began with the magazine interview, which was when he'd first had suspicions about Felicia and took Lucy through everything that had happened to him since he'd last seen her earlier that afternoon. She listened without comment and didn't ask any questions. When he ran out of words, he just stopped talking.

There was so much more to say, but he no longer trusted his verbal skills. *I want you* was too weak and easily misunderstood. *I love you* too trite and overused. *I need you* too small and ineffectual. He crossed his arms to keep from touching her and *showing* her all of the things that lived and burned deep inside him.

Lucy couldn't believe what he'd been through tonight. She'd come so close to losing him. Too close. Since the beginning of their marriage she'd been the one in jeopardy. He'd been the one to protect her. And now when he'd needed her the most, she'd been curled up in a ball too afraid to look past what she'd seen to what she *knew*. Too scared to trust when all he'd given her was an open road to trust him. He'd *earned* her trust, and she'd refused to give it, holding on tight to it as though she needed for an escape hatch, a way out when things got too hard.

She was ashamed of herself. This man loved her and their daughter. He took care of them and cared for them. He was everything she wanted and needed. All she had to do was trust him.

"She could've killed you." Saying it out loud made the backs of her eyes sting.

"I thought for a moment she might," he said. "All the

while I kept thanking God that you and Poppy weren't here."

"I wish I'd been here."

"No, darlin', you don't. I didn't have anything to lose when I grabbed for that gun. If you'd have been here, well, that would've complicated things considerably. I would've had *everything* to lose."

"I never really listened to you when you said things like that to me. I heard the words, but I didn't take them in. And you've backed up those words at every turn. I can't think of one time where your words didn't match your actions. If only I'd paid attention. If I'd only taken it all in. I *do* owe you an apology, Cal, for not believing you when you told me there was nothing between you and Felicia. Because I knew it. Deep inside I knew it."

"What are you saying?"

"I'm saying that I know you didn't cheat on me. That you've never cheated on me during our marriage and that you never will cheat. I'm hoping you can forgive me for not trusting you. And I'm really hoping that you're happy about this baby." She took his hand and laid it across her belly. "Because I can't have this baby without you, Cal Sellers. I just can't." She burst into tears, and before she knew it he had her wrapped up tight against him.

"Am I happy? Oh, darlin'. When you told me in my office about the baby, it was a kick to the gut after a beating. All I kept thinking was how I'd lost the right to be there with you, how I wouldn't get to see my children every day. I thought I'd lost you all forever. I'm happy. I'm so damn ecstatic I can hardly hold it in."

"Really?"

He cupped her face and grinned down at her. "Really, darlin'. *Really*."

"Can I...? Can I stay here tonight?"

"You can stay wherever you like."

"I want to sleep in our bed. With you right next to me. I want to wake up wrapped in your arms, and I want to burn through a couple of options. If you're up to it."

"I'm up to all of that."

"Then what are you waiting for, cowboy?"

He scooped her up off the couch and took the stairs two at a time. "This, darlin', is going to be option number fifty-five."

*

Thank you for reading REAL! The next book in the DANGEROUS LINES series is URGE .

With danger closing in, will Cal and Lucy make it or will her ex get to her first?

➤**CLICK HERE TO READ URGE**

If you enjoyed FAKE, please consider leaving a review on your favorite book site. Reviews help readers find books!

➤REAL (A LOVE STORIES novel)

➤GOODREADS

Join my VIP Facebook group Babes with Books for exclusive sneak peeks at my upcoming books & other, members only, perks:

➤www.facebook.com/groups/BabesWithBooksReaderGroup

Sign up to receive my newsletter for new release alerts, exclusive bonus content, and giveaways!

➤**www.bethyarnall.com/newsletter**

Turn the page to read an excerpt from URGE now!

EXCERPT FROM URGE

There weren't a great many things that bothered Erin December. For the most part, she considered herself a pretty even-keeled person. So why was her face hot and the back of her throat aching with the words she couldn't let loose? As she sat in the Kavender Investments staff meeting, listening to Ramie Kavender heap praise on Austin for the success of the Petrie project, she couldn't believe what she was hearing. That son of a bitch Austin accepted the compliments as if they were his due, never once daring to glance her direction or acknowledge that she had any part in the project, let alone admitting she had done the bulk of the work.

She reminded herself that she was grateful for the job. The tiny town of San Rey, in central California, had been hit hard by the downturn in the economy. Kavender Investments was one of the few companies thriving amongst speculation of another recession. Without this job, she might be forced to leave the town she grew up in and move to a bigger town like Santa Barbara or Los Angeles. She liked her job and most of the people she worked with. She was confident in her work in a way she'd never been in any other position she'd ever held.

But that didn't mean she liked being stepped on by Austin on his way to a higher title.

As soon as the meeting was over, she escaped to the relative quiet of her cubicle. She pulled up the report she'd been working on before the meeting began and started to recheck the data one last time before she turned it in. A shadow fell over her.

"I have a favor to ask," her boss Ramie said.

She turned in her chair.

"Chelsea went home sick. She had a Cash for Keys appointment this afternoon at four. Can you take it? Should be quick. You can go straight home from there."

That was in half an hour and she still had the report to finish. "Sure."

"Thanks. I owe you one." He dropped the folder on the top of her already teetering stack and strode away.

She suppressed a sigh and reached for the file. The tab had the name Lasiter on it. She knew a Greg Lasiter from high school. Opening the file, she confirmed that it was *the* Greg Lasiter she'd be meeting with. Great. Just great. He was an asshole back then and while he didn't waste time picking on her anymore, he wasn't exactly nice.

The words in the file blurred, then blacked over. Her body seemed to shoot back as though she were on a rollercoaster, pain searing between her eyes. The sensation made her stomach dip. She knew what this was. She hadn't experienced this loss of control since she'd first come into her ability when she was eight. Shoved suddenly from one reality into another against her will, she found herself standing on the front porch of the Lasiter house. She worked to steady her breathing. Leaves danced across the lawn, the wind whipping them up, then sending them scattering.

What was happening?

She hadn't called up this vision. She hadn't chosen to be here in this time or this place. Trying to get her bearings, she glanced back at the neighborhood she'd walked through once upon a time on her way to and from elementary school. The street was empty.

She never used her ability. Ever. Only her Aunt Cerie and her father, Donald, knew what she could do. She kept it that way on purpose, holding her secret inside since the night her mother had left and never came back.

In the vision she was herself, knocking on the door of the Lasiter house, calling out for Greg. No answer. She pushed the doorbell and rapped on the door again. Silence. She shuddered from a chill she couldn't feel. Something was off.

Not real, she reminded herself. Her body still sat at her desk, but her mind had traveled through time. Was this the past or future? Why was she here? *How* did she get here? What did this loss of control over her ability mean?

Turning the knob, she expected it to be locked, but it turned easily. She walked into an empty living room, stripped of furniture or anything that made it a home.

"Greg?" she heard herself call out. "It's Erin December from Kavender Investments. Hello? Anyone here?"

A light around a door at the end of the living room drew her attention. Her steps weighted, she found she couldn't stop. Any of it. Not her body from moving forward nor her mind from staying in the vision. She was stuck. Left with no choice. She closed her eyes, using the tools she'd been taught to search for a way out. But there was no ending it. The shock of that radiated through her.

This had never happened before either. She'd *always* been able to pull out of a vision.

She put a hand out and opened the door. It swung away, revealing a small kitchen. Greg lay on the floor face up, a pool of blood around him.

He was dead.

She gasped and stumbled back.

As abruptly as she was sucked into the vision, she was spit right back out. She dragged in air, gripping the edge of her desk. *It wasn't real. It wasn't real.*

The file still lay open on her desk. The office seemed to go on about its business around her, oblivious to what she'd just gone through. She pulled her phone out to call her aunt to tell her what had happened and saw the time. A quarter to four. She had fifteen minutes to get to Greg's house. Greg. She should call for someone to save him. She punched in 9-1 then hesitated, her thumb hovering over the second one. What would she say? Who would believe her if she told them what she'd seen in her vision?

She wasn't supposed to use her ability to change the future. That lesson had been drummed into her at an early age, from the first flickers of her ability asserting itself. If she changed one thing, it could potentially change a thousand little things. A man was dead. Or would be dead. Certainly there were exceptions. But wouldn't saving him be the absolute worst-case scenario? Could she live with herself if she did nothing? What choice was there?

She put on her coat and grabbed her purse and the Lasiter file. There was something wrong with her ability for sure. It was out of whack, totally out of her control. Maybe it wasn't true. Maybe her vision was wrong. *Please let it be wrong.*

She pushed through the door of the building where Kavender Investments had offices and onto Main Street. The people of San Rey went about their day. She envied them. She'd never wanted her ability, never wanted to be marked as different. She'd only ever wanted to fit in. Born into a family that didn't hide who they were, Erin felt like an outcast there too, keeping her ability a secret and never using it. She passed through town, attracting her usual amount of odd stares and whispers. She was used to it, but today she challenged their stares, glaring back when she would've glanced away.

Greg couldn't be dead.

Quickening her pace, she kept an eye on the sky, which seemed to increase its threat of rain with every step she took. It was the kind of sky her superstitious Aunt Cerie called volcanic, a portent of violence. Erin didn't subscribe to her aunt's superstitions, but she certainly wished she hadn't left her umbrella in her car, and her car with her aunt. That's what Erin got for loaning it to Cerie and for wearing suede heels on a day with a forty percent chance of rain.

Couldn't she catch a break just once?

She gripped the leather handle of her bag tighter as she broke into a jog, hoping to get to the house before the sky opened up. Not that she was in any hurry to get there. She passed homes, some vacant, some close enough that they'd taken on the same hollowed out look. The economic downturn had hit San Rey especially hard.

She opened the front gate of Greg Lasiter's house, releasing the leaves stuck to it, and slowly made her way up the front walk. At the door, she hesitated and prepared herself for the reality of the images that had assailed her when she'd touched the property file. A simple Cash for Keys, Ramie had said.

But nothing was ever simple in Erin's world.

Taking a deep breath, she knocked. If her vision were true, no one would answer. *Please let Greg answer.* Brushing the shards of flaked gate paint from her fingers, she was tempted to just pull out her cell phone and place the call she'd started at the office. But that's not how it worked. If her vision was real, the scene had to play out exactly as she'd seen it.

Clutching her bag tighter under her arm, she knocked again. "Hello? Mr. Lasiter? It's Erin from Kavender Investments."

She felt stupid calling him Mr. Lasiter instead of Greg. He was only a year older than she was. She'd had a stupid unrequited crush on him her freshman year of high school. And now she was standing on his dilapidated porch, supposedly waiting for him to open the door so she could take the keys to his home. The home he'd grown up in. She shouldn't feel guilty about that and yet she did.

"Mr. Lasiter?" She rapped on the door again. "Hello?"

Inside, the house was silent. Outside, the only sound was the whoosh of wind, lifting the curling ends of her brown hair, bringing with it the briny tinge of the ocean and a chill that bit right through her wool coat. Just like her vision. If Erin was smart she'd follow her instincts and run back the way she'd come. But she had her father's practicality and a bank balance that didn't allow for fear.

She had to see this through.

Still no answer. She'd hoped so hard that what she'd seen would be as wrong as the way it had come to her. She closed her eyes and silently chanted the words of protection she'd been taught as a child, mentally drawing a shield around herself. Focusing her energy, she took three deep breaths, letting each of them out slowly, preparing herself for the possible reality of what she'd only seen in her mind.

She opened her eyes and turned the knob. Locked. She hadn't expected that. Her visions *never* wavered. For a moment, she didn't know what to do. The wrongness poked at her.

Careful what you wish for.

Maybe there was a key. She searched the usual places —under the doormat, above the door, the light fixture, a dead potted plant—there.

Dusting the dirt from the key, she revealed a floral pattern. It was one of those novelty keys Fine's Hardware had started carrying some time back. Erin had one herself. She dug her key ring from her pocket and compared the near identical house keys. The irony wasn't lost on her. If it wasn't for her job with Kavender Investments, Austin or Ramie himself might have knocked on her door with a check to exchange for the key to *her* house.

She pocketed her keys once again and fit the dirt-smudged key from the planter into the lock. It fit, turning easily in the knob. The door creaked on rusty hinges, the curse of coastal living.

"Hello? Mr. Lasiter?" Her voice echoed off the walls of the near empty room.

Daylight made a weak effort to invade the space, casting no shadows. It was colder here, but not cold enough to mist her breath. The air lay still and ripe with wariness, as though the house had not yet made up its mind to accept her. Or maybe she was the one who refused to accept what had been so clear in her vision.

She didn't want to go into the house, didn't want to be the one to make the discovery.

The layout was different from what she'd seen in her mind. Almost a mirror image, except for a door where there should have been a hall, and a fireplace where there should've been none. The differences were disorienting. It took her a moment to get her bearings. Different. Everything was so *different* from what she'd seen.

Why? What does it mean?

She called out for Greg again. No answer. She should leave. Right now. But her feet propelled her farther into the room as if controlled by someone or something else.

She swallowed at the lump of dread in her throat. She'd been drawn to the door at the far end of the room just like her vision and now there, standing before it, she couldn't seem to stop her shaking hand from reaching out to open it. A noise from the other side made her flinch.

She swung the door open slowly, revealing the room inches at a time. "Greg? It's me, Erin, fr—" She let go of the knob, clamping both hands to her mouth. The door continued on its own, exposing the scene.

Greg knelt over the body of a woman sprawled out on the floor in a thin pool of blood.

Behind him, the kitchen wall was dotted and streaked with more blood. He slowly raised his gaze.

"I didn't do it." He swayed back and forth. His eyes, dull with shock, stayed on Erin's. "I didn't do it."

*

★ URGE is a 2016 Daphne du Maurier contest winner★

Want to read more?

➤One-click Urge Now➤

If you loved REAL, you'll love the sexy, funny, award nominated INNOCENT serial. Cora's brother was convicted of a murder he didn't commit and it's up to her to set him free. Inspired by real cases taken on by The Innocence Project.

★ Nominated in 2017 for the Romance Writers of America Rita® award★

➤One-click EPISODE ONE Now➤

Looking for something lighter and funny? Check out THE MISADVENTURES OF MAGGIE MAE series, starting with WAKE UP, MAGGIE, available now! Maggie has to keep her very inappropriate thoughts to herself about the FBI Special Agent assigned to protect her from a murderer.

➤One-click WAKE UP, MAGGIE Now➤

HAVE YOU BEEN ABUSED?

Your safety is important. *You're* important.

Help is available 24/7 by telephone and online.

The National Domestic Abuse Hotline

If you or someone you know is experiencing domestic violence there is help through the National Domestic Abuse hotline. Trained advocates are available to take your calls toll free, 24/7 hotline at 1-800-799-SAFE (7233).

Donations to support the hotline can be made at www.thehotline.org.

RAINN

The National Sexual Assault Online Hotline

Your privacy and safety are crucial. Please make sure you are in a safe place and that you are using a secure device and Internet connection. Please note that while we have taken numerous measures to keep your communications safe while using our site, no Internet transmission is 100% secure.

Chat online with a trained staff member who can provide you confidential crisis support.

www.rainn.org
or by phone
1-888-656-HOPE (4673)

ALSO BY BETH YARNALL

Dangerous Lines

Lost

Saved

Fake

Real

Urge

Rare

Betray

Recovered Innocence

Liberate

Exonerate

Vindicate

Innocent Serial

Episode One

Episode Two

Episode Three

The Misadventures of Maggie Mae

Wake Up, Maggie

You're Mine, Maggie

Find Me, Maggie

Azalea March Mysteries

Dyed and Gone

Beth Writing as Betty Paper

Exposed

Captive

Tinsel

Piano Lessons

BETH'S BOOKS FOR WRITERS

Crafting Unputdownable Fiction series
Going Deep Into Deep Point of View
Making Description Work Hard For You
Some Like It Hot: Writing Sex and Romance

ACKNOWLEDGMENTS

I'm grateful for my family who supports my writing career and especially for my sons who get teased about the sexy books their mom writes. Sorry boys. Just try to remember that each books gets us that much closer to the pool you want. My thanks to my mom and my sister, who are the last set of eagle eyes to review all of my books before publication. Any mistakes are totally theirs not mine. To the fine women of The Keeper Shelf—the mighty, mighty unicorns—you are truly my New York.

ABOUT THE AUTHOR

USA Today best selling author and Rita® finalist, Beth Yarnall, writes mysteries, romantic suspense, and the occasional hilarious tweet. She lives in Southern California with her husband, two sons, and their rescue dogs where she is hard at work on her next novel. For more information about Beth and her novels please visit her website- www.bethyarnall.com

🅕 facebook.com/bethyarnallauthor

ⓐ amazon.com/author/bethyarnall

BB bookbub.com/authors/beth-yarnall